Ink of Ebony: The Essence of Womanhood

AJ Brown, Frania G. Romulus, La'Risa Black,
Mattison H. Bond, Monai the Poet, Sarah Alayne
Martin, thatqu33nshae, Winifred Summer

Sovereign Noire Media

Contents

Chapter 1
Joy | thatqu33nshae

T hatqu33nshae was born Sheryl Raleigh in the Bronx, NY. She currently resides in South Carolina where she owns theThatqu33nshae Enterprises LLC. She began writing poetry at a young age but didn't become serious about her poetry until the age of 33 when she started performing spoken word in Greensboro, NC and joined Instagram in 2022.

Sheryl is the creator and host of The Healing Room on Instagram. She was blessed to become a member and board member of The Galaxy of Poets and works diligently to increase awareness of mental health and domestic abuse in her community.

***

This piece was written at a time when I realized that my joy is the love that I give to others and not of anything material. I spent so much time looking for dormant validation and through therapy, I realized that the joy and validation I was searching in all the wrong places for was in me all along.

JOY

Hello joy nice to see you again

I apologize for being away so long it's good to see you my friend

We could sit and talk about the memories of when

But so much has happened since then

I spent so much time trying to find the key to release you

I searched for years through and through

I spent years in depression

Learned a plethora of lessons

Never forgot each breath I took was a blessing

Giving and giving until I was drained

Never thought to quit or complain

I finally got tired of the pain

Decided to make a change

I moved away and rearranged my way of living and thinking

No longer was I sinking

After taking time to grow

Tilling the ground of my heart for seeds to sow

I watered my garden with tears

From an overflowing dam prepared for years

The blossoming flowers revealed to me

That all the love I've been carrying was always the key

So welcome back to my life

I'll never again lose sight

No one will ever again destroy

My desire to share my love with the world

The key to my joy

Chapter 2
Side Effects | AJ Brown

AJ Brown is a North Carolina native. She is the author of the poetry book, *LoveLetters Never Sent To: Myself.* She is also the creator and host of the podcast, "Here's What's Going On". She is also currently completing her Bachelor's Degree in Computer Science. AJ always finds the time to do what she loves, which includes reading and writing poetry, YA fiction, and screenwriting movies and TV shows. AJ uses her trauma to give voice to the little black girls that grow into adult black women that feel they have no voice in a society that uses them for entertainment but doesn't care to hear their truth.

> *Being featured will assist in supporting my writing career by giving my work a place to be understood and seen by people like me. This is a great platform for my work to be represented without the cost of being stolen or misused.*

Side Effects is about how a young black woman and her family cope with the loss of her younger sister. The side effects of loss are something everyone knows or will know eventually, but when loss happens unexpectedly and the people responsible don't get the justice they deserve, it can cause self-destruction.

Side Effects

[FLASHBACK. EXT/INT. MORGUE - WAITING ROOM - MID MORNING]

Off-white walls of the waiting area shrink the room, a fluorescent light bulb dims and goes out. A row of five lightly padded steel chairs sit separately against three walls of the room. A medium sized cheap wooden coffee table sits in the middle of the room with popular magazines on it.

Lou sits on the edge of her chair, her leg bouncing, with her eyes closed, she inhales through her mouth and exhales through her nose slowly.

LOU/LOUTRINA CARTER, early twenties. She grew up too quick, was a child too little and compromises herself for people that don't deserve it, deserve her.

GABE

Ms. Carter?

GABE, mid-fifties, medical examiner, kind eyes like Santa Claus, overly soothing voice.

Lou stands up, her hands in the pocket of her oversized hoodie. Gabe extends his hand for Lou to shake.

LOU

Lou...Lou's good.

Lou removes her hands from her hoodie pocket, swiftly wipes them on her jeans, she shakes Gabe's hand.

GABE

I'm Gabe, we're ready for you, but first I would like to prepare you for—

LOU

(Nervously) I'm good, I've ran through dis in my head and I've—I'm good.

Gabe nods and smiles lightly at Lou, he turns around and Lou follows after him down a brightly lit hallway.

[INT. MORGUE VIEWING ROOM]

Lou stares down at the white sheeted body on the metal table of the well brightly lit room, tears brimming her eyes, hands clutched together in front of her face.

GABE

Okay, I'll just explain that you'll be identifying whom we believe to be Vanessa Penning, her relation to you, your sister.

Lou nods her head once and exhales, her shoulders hunching.

Gabe walks toward the sheeted body and turns around to Lou.

GABE

There is some bruising around her face, as well as minor cuts, we've cleaned her up as well as we could. You can stay for however long you would like.

Lou nods her head and closes her eyes taking in a large inhale.

Gabe turns to the metal table and begins to fold down the white sheet revealing the head area down to the top of the shoulders of the body. He steps away and stands aside, hands clasped in front of him.

Lou opens her eyes and stares down at the body, tears fall down her face, she wipes them away with her sleeve covered hands.

GABE

Is this Vanessa Penning?

Lou nods.

GABE

I need verbal confirmation.

LOU

(Whispers) Yes.

Lou glances away from Ness' body to Gabe.

LOU

(Whispers) Can I touch her?

GABE

Yes, here.

Gabe steps forward untucking the sheet revealing Ness' hand and steps back and walks to the corner of the room and removes a file from the desk, he opens it and begins to write.

Lou hesitates but steps forward taking Ness' hand rubbing her thumb over the ring indention.

LOU

Where's her stuff, her jewelry and stuff?

Gabe closes the file, placing it back down on the desk, he stares at Lou adjusting his glasses.

GABE

They're being held. Since the manner in which your sister was found has been deemed as a crime her belongings are evidence.

Lou shakes her head, she leans forward and caresses Vanessa's hair, tears fall down her cheeks as she gazes at the severe bruising of Ness' face, the broken bright colored nails on her hand.

Lou takes Ness' hand in her hands, she collapses to her knees sobbing still holding Ness' hand.

[BACK TO PRESENT DAY. EXT/INT. OFFICE BUILDING - THERAPIST OFFICE - DAY]

AUGUST

Lou?

Lou wipes the tears from her face, reaching into her pocket for her vape pen, she takes a hit from it and blows out the smoke blankly staring at August.

LOU

She said shit, I said shit, I shoulda neva done dat.

AUGUST

Are you being honest or just saying that because it's the right thing to say?

LOU

Does it matta? This is STUPID, I'm here for no reason.

AUGUST

No, you're here because you attacked your mother and assaulted her and tried to kill yourself.

Lou smiles, smirks, breaks out into laughter. She glances down at her wrist.

LOU

(Laughing) Horizontal for attention, vertical for results.

August stares at Lou, serious and sympathetic.

AUGUST

What does that mean?

Lou's head lulls to the side, her eyes gazing at August.

LOU

Nothin', something Rocky says—it's a joke.

AUGUST

She attempted suicide too, right?

LOU

You got all my shit in that file huh?

AUGUST

You found her.

LOU

Saved her.

AUGUST

How old were you?

LOU

I don't remember.

AUGUST

You saved Rocky's life.

LOU

What was left of it.

AUGUST

Do you talk to Rocky?

LOU

Yeah.

AUGUST

You close with her?

LOU

Now.

AUGUST

You weren't always close?

LOU

No. She was...Rocky's different.

AUGUST

How is she different?

Lou sits forward in her seat running her hand through her purple and black faux locs.

LOU

I don't know—just different!

AUGUST

How close are you and Rocky now?

LOU

Close enough?

AUGUST

Do you see her often?

LOU

Yeah, she's staying wit' Amoomoo, our grandma, now.

AUGUST

Do you feel numb when you're with Rocky?

Lou wraps her arms around herself gazing at the floor.

LOU

(Faintly) I try not to. I mean...I've always felt like that, but I could...I could manage it betta.

AUGUST

When's the first time you can remember when you felt numb?

Lou looks up at August smirking.

LOU

"I was just born broken." Jora used to say that to me all the time when I'd—

AUGUST

Who's Jora?

LOU

(Sarcastically) She not in your notes?

August smiles lightly at Lou and shakes her head.

LOU

Ray's mom.

AUGUST

Your paternal grandma.

Lou nods once at August then glances back at the floor.

AUGUST

You see her often?

Lou relaxes back into the chair shaking her head gazing back at August taking a hit from her vape pen.

LOU

She's been dead ova five years.

AUGUST

You miss her?

LOU

Yeah, sure. She use ta babysit me and my cousin Bishop.

AUGUST

How old were you then?

LOU

Five or six, I don't remember?

AUGUST

She watched you both while Cassandra and your dad went to work or?

LOU

Yeah, and if Milly was sick.

AUGUST

He was sick a lot?

LOU

Yup.

AUGUST

He's been sick since he was child?

LOU

Since he was born. He has congenital heart and lung defect.

AUGUST

He's still dealing with his condition?

LOU

No—yeah-I mean—he gotta heart transplant, but they had complications, he got a lung infection in both lungs and scar tissue—he's...he's on the lung transplant list now.

AUGUST

Must be difficult to watch your brother go through so much?

Lou shrugs her shoulders taking a deep inhale/exhale.

LOU

I don't have to deal with it really.

AUGUST

You ever go visit him in the hospital as child?

LOU

When they let me.

AUGUST

How often did you get to go?

LOU

(Annoyed) Oh my gawd bruh, dis is stupid.

Lou yawns reaching into her scrub top pocket removing her cell phone staring at the screen.

LOU

You got ten more minutes.

AUGUST

I'm aware of the time.

Lou nods her head in approval of August's response.

AUGUST

You went to live with your dad after Cassandra kicked you out?

LOU

No, not at first. I lived in my car for a while, then Milly found out and told Ray, he made me move in with them.

AUGUST

So, it's alright to call Ray your dad?

LOU

Technically he is. He ain't always been there, but he's been there when I needed' em.

AUGUST

You're living with him and his wife.

LOU

Sandé.

AUGUST

That's his wife?

LOU

Yeah, I call her mom.

AUGUST

You're close with her?

LOU

Yeah, she's been around since I was little.

AUGUST

You talk to her a lot?

LOU

Sometimes. I work a lot.

AUGUST

Right, at the nursing home. Still planning to go back to school?

LOU

After I get my car fixed.

AUGUST

What would you go back to school for?

LOU

To become a registered nurse.

AUGUST

Why that?

LOU

Already a CNA, might as well.

AUGUST

You ever make definitive decisions about anything in your life, or do you always just go with the flow?

LOU

Life does what it wants to you anyway, what's the point in tryin to prevent somethin I can't?

AUGUST

Is that how you feel about Ness dying, that you could have prevented it?

LOU

No, that was fate.

AUGUST

So, it was fate that the court ruled the way they did in her case?

Lou glares at August, pained by her comment.

LOU

No!

AUGUST

How can that be any different?

Lou sits forward in her seat staring August down clenching her fist clearly aggravated.

LOU

Because it is.

AUGUST

How so?

LOU

Because it just is!

Lou stares down August shaking with rage.

[EXT. OUTSIDE OFFICE BUILDING - DAY]

Lou storms from the office building down the sidewalk, her fist clenched vaping from her vape pen. A random stranger fans away the large puff of smoke from Lou's vape pen.

Chapter 3
Love is in Janette...ikz | Monai the Poet

M onai the Poet is an author of poetry and flash fiction as well as a blog writer and aspiring artist. Born in Pittsburgh, PA she currently resides in Lithonia, Georgia as a child-care educator and art instructor.

Her current project is a blog entitled "the Writings of Monai the Poet" which provides poetry and essay testimonies of her faith. In addition to her published poetry book "Flawed Human, Loved Soul" she is published in an anthology called *Crossing Borders* with a story entitled "Killing Him with Kindness". She also has a short story published in Adelaide Literary Magazine called "Bad Coffee". She obtained an Associate's Degree in Creative Writing through Full Sail University. Monai works freelance with different writing projects, including a poetic script for an up-and-coming docuseries. Her visual arts mediums include acrylic painting, resin art, pottery, and sketching.

Of all things in the realm of creativity her strongest love is poetry, following a line of strong women poets in the generations before her. Her aspirations are to live as a vessel of Christ and serve as a creative to spread the Gospel and love to uplift and inspire others.

***

I want to acknowledge a woman who's been pivotal in my growth as a poet, spoken word artist and woman of God. I want her and others to know how influential she's been in my life and honor her for continuing to be an advocate for other writers and creatives.

This poem is dedicated to musician, poet and dancer Janette Watson, known to most as Janette...ikz or iamgenetics. I've had the privilege to not only be blessed by her poetry and testimony in the Christian faith but also as a student and mentee of hers. Upon meeting her, I began to learn more about her as a woman of God, a mother and a creative. Through that time she has taught and encouragement in the realm of creativity and courage but also just as a black Christian woman living in today's society where living under the calling of artistic expression is rarely acknowledged or credited. She has blessed many people with her powerful words but also in kindness and honesty.

I want to take this opportunity to acknowledge her for her humbleness, selflessness and strength, simply because she's a woman who has unmatched modesty and integrity. As I've witnessed her being a light to those around her I felt it only fitting to honor the God who blessed us with her.

Love is in Janette...ikz

Ode to Janette

The first time I met you

I fangirled

Scared to know if I

Ever made it obvious

That seeing you in the flesh

Spun me to fantasy fiction and back

You were a celebrity to me

So when someone asked me

If I met anyone famous in Atlanta

I thought of you and said yes

The first piece I'd ever heard of yours

Was a first for many

You talked about waiting

For your man of God and

No longer settling with a simpleton

You were a vessel of conviction

And hope all at once

Your words punched new passion

Into my lungs to write again

To believe again

Every lyrical testimony since

Was a seed sewn in the soil

Of my faith

Watered by our righteous gardener

You flourished on good ground

Even when those watching

Were ignorant to the environment in which

Weather conditions tried to stifle your growth

Like Maya Angelou

Still you rose

It's one thing to know the poet

And the musician

Another to meet the teacher

The mother and the friend

The more your petals of wisdom

Dropped seeds in our fertile ignorance

The more we saw you wither

And be reborn

As if your soul could radiate more light

You are unaware of the blessing you are

Remnants of motherhood

Adorn your neck in a garland of grace

Even when you only see

Garlands of tiredness draped under your eyes

And weakness covering your melanin

More than your tattoos

Yet even when your stride breaks

You dress your stress

Your presence is pleasant though

Life constantly presents unpleasantness

You are still mysterious

Taking orders with gems sparkling through the smile

You forget you have

I often wonder if you know you are adored

Not because your dedication

To servitude is foreign to strangers

Reaching for handouts

Or your talent creates snaps and claps in our souls

But because your love for Christ

Is evident in each of your actions

Ready or not

You let us into your crayon box

When God told you

Red was still your favorite color

Sobs filled my broken spirit

As he brought it back to being mine

You don't know how your openness

Closed all doors to any doubt

That you are who God said you are

And He is who he says He is

To God I give my gratitude for you

A submissive vessel that is teaching me

What it means to rejoice in suffering

That obedience to love others as yourself

Is not impossible with God

That every good and perfect gift from above

Can be stewarded well even in brokenness

That in the pursuit of greatness

Love exists

In you I've witnessed

All that to say

Blessed

Grateful

Humble I stay

To see you as an abundantly gifted human

Sitting in the guiding hand of God

But to know you as friend

As mentor

As auntie

As Janette

Chapter 4
Crossroads | Sarah Alayne Martin

S arah Alayne Martin is a Black poet, storyteller, radical communicator, and budding healer with roots in the South and the Midwest. She is a 2022 Anaphora Poetry fellow as well as a grantee of the Young Black Climate Leaders Youth Futures Fund. Finding inspiration from nature and her own lived experiences, Sarah's poetic musings and short stories are an invitation to restore, reconnect, and reclaim our intrinsic ways of being. Ultimately, her art casts spells, offering spiritual ascension and opening portals to other worlds. You can check out Sarah's most recent published piece, "Finding Freedom on the Other Side of the Waterfall" in Spoken Black Girl Magazine. To read more of Sarah's writing, connect with her on Instagram at @poeticportals.

***

I've been thinking a lot about how people talk about the importance of giving Black women their flowers while they are here instead of when they pass, and I am a firm supporter of this. But I also believe one of the best gifts you can give to another Black woman is the gift of rest. So "Crossroads" is an invitation to Black women to rest now as a way of celebrating ourselves. Alluding to Lucille Clifton's work, "won't you celebrate with me," I begin my poem with a similar rhetorical question: "Won't you come, / come as you are / and join me at the / foot of the dirt road, / carved lovingly by / Grandma's hands." Similar to Clifton's work there is a weariness here, but also an element of celebration. What if Black women were celebrated for taking rest now instead of when they pass? What if Black women could rejoice in rest together? These are the questions this poem explores.

Crossroads

Won't you come,

come as you are

and join me at the

foot of the dirt road,

carved lovingly by

Grandma's hands.

Won't you wipe the

dirt from tired eyes

and peer into the river

waters, flowing next

to the bank. With three

eyes open, won't you

see your highest self

clearly? Won't you let

your midnight coated

limbs dance freely in the

moonlight, rest assured

of your holiness. Won't

you lay your body down

on a bed of stars, plucked

from the meadow. Won't

you come to repose in

the self? With us.

Won't you?

Chapter 5
Rejoice | Mattison H. Bond

M attison H. Bond is a storyteller. A writer. A public historian and librarian. She is a black woman, born and bred in the beautiful rural south of North Eastern North Carolina. She is a lover of God. A lover of good music and good food. She loves people, black people, and women (because she is all three). Influenced by the greats, Toni Morrison, Alice Walker, Zora Neale Hurston, she writes about black folks from rural areas like herself. If she is not writing slow poetic fiction, she is creating new worlds influenced by her study and love of history. And if she is not doing that, she is pushing forward within her career as a public historian and librarian, researching and constantly reading. She received her undergraduate degree in history from the Elizabeth City State University and is currently writing her thesis to graduate from North Carolina Central with a Master's in History.

***

Deep in the countryside sits an old church on a hill. Courtnee, a member of this church, remembers it with nothing but feelings of family and love. But as with most things, even this church has changed. Courtnee is no longer the young girl and the church is no longer as she left it. She learns from this experience that even though things get old, there are some things that will never fade away.

Rejoice

Courtnee grew up inside a church. She remembered the summer when the rain beat harder than the feet of the congregation, singing along with the choir as they were "doing their thang!" as her father often said. Everyone huddled in, silent and praying the summer rain did not turn into anything that could harm their little haven on the hill. Three women, hair and dresses wet, would stand at the front of the church. The sound of their feet forcefully beat against the ground. They sang, loudness cutting through the air. A smile on their faces, as if the song ushered in memories of nights when they thought all was lost, but He was able to find.

After the song ended there was a buzzing energy in the church. It jumped from shoulder to large, flowered hat. It invited someone to stand up and say a prayer, to tell the congregation how good He's been! Courtnee's favorite part was when her Aunt Joyce would sing. She was larger than life and brown as tobacco. She sang the sorrows that life had given her or the joy that God had decided she was worthy enough to receive. And everyone in that church would sway or clap or "Amen" to the sound of her voice.

Church was different now.

No longer did the red brick stand out from the countryside. It molded into the heat, at one with the wide dead field that surrounded the church. The bricks were dirty. The doors were new. She pushed them open, they made no sound just like the floors. She wondered how the choir would keep to beat with the organ player. Her wondering stopped at the sight of a cream and black drum set.

Her pew was still empty and welcoming. Everyone she knew seemed to float toward the same seats. Everyone she did not know, she wondered who they were and where did they come from. She sat down, touching her aunt's shoulder and smiling in that warm way she was taught to all those years ago. But before her aunt could turn herself to return the hello, the organ started to sing small and shy notes, and the drummer confidently silenced the sanctuary.

The doors to the fellowship hall flew open and the ministers of the church walked in. She wondered when they had all gotten matching robes, and who had taught them to smile in such a tight dignified way, as if they were smiling down, pitying them. Next, her eyes caught the bright colors of long church robes and gold chains hanging off the small frame of a dark man. He raised his arms, palms opened, and people began to clap. Others laughed, as if joy had just come in the morning. And when the man took his place in the center of the pulpit, hands gripping the gold lined podium, she knew this was the pastor. He looked out of place among them, like the new wide screen televisions that hung on each side at the front of the church.

Four women walked in. Their heads down, they followed an unfamiliar woman. She was colored just as brightly as the pastor, her head held high and only she held the mic. She opened her mouth wide to sing, and out came an unamplified voice. She patted the top of the mic with a manicured hand. No sound. Panic appeared around her eyes. A few people in the crowd whispered and looked on.

And then her Aunt Joyce began to sing. Her hands held the rounded edge of the pew and her back straightened. She tilted her head back and started to push sweet air out of her lungs.

"I thank the Loorrrdddd, for alllll he's done."

The church became quiet, and the air seemed to leave the sanctuary. Everyone looked toward the pastor and waited. He stood, clutching the gold podium, sweat forming on his forehead. Even on his dark skin, she saw the red of frustration, of anger, brightening. Someone began to clap. Aunt Joyce rocked to the beat of her stomping foot. Her mother then started to respond to the call.

"I thank the lord—"

"Yes, I thank the lord."

"For all he's done—"

"Yes, I thank the Lord."

Courtnee began to sing along. Her hands met each other in the sweet familiarity of a resounding clap. The smack of feet against the floor began to bounce off the walls and into the empty spaces of the church. The organist leaned forward, playing the notes that ushered in amens and hallelujahs since her youth. The pastor, furious, went over to the organist. He starts to yell and waves his hands, motioning to the ministers to do something! One of them jumps down from the pulpit, yelling at the organist. The drummer picks up his sticks, only to have them slapped away by some unseen force. In desperation the pastor leans over to pull the plug of the old organ. He looks up only to notice the organist still feverishly playing on the keys, clapping in between notes and singing with the rest of the congregation.

Then the floors started to quake. The walls shook off its dust. And the ceiling cracked, throwing plaster toward the floor. The pastor jumped out of the way and the newcomers covered their heads with hymnals, running for cover, outside into the lifeless fields

And there, within the quaking walls of that little old church, Courtnee looked around to see divine joy on the faces of all the people she called family. The music, the sound of many feet and clapping hands, moved the oldest member into a lively dance. She danced like her feet had touched the ground for the first time. She never missed a step, even when the large, shiny, new televisions shattered behind her. The glass flying into the flowers on her hat. And her Aunt Joyce continued to rock in her pew, head back, singing to the God that had preserved her and brought her nothing but joy.

Chapter 6
Characteristics of Conjure Expression | La'Risa Black

I am a Brooklyn native who has transplanted to Atlanta to pursue education. I have a Bachelor of Arts in English from Clark Atlanta University and a Master's in Public Administration from Kennesaw State University. By day, I am an elementary Exceptional Education teacher. I am also a Ph.D. candidate in the Humanities program at Clark Atlanta University, where my concentrations are Africana Women's Studies and English. Specifically, my area of expertise is *Black Women's use of Conjure as a Liberatory Practice.* Outside work and school, I am a Spiritualist, Hoodoo Practitioner, Tarot Reader, and my Community's Conjure Woman!

***

Inspired by Zora Neale Hurston's, Characteristics of Negro Expression, and The Wiz, this composition provides insight into some ways the elements may be used to conjure. Supporting the theme of rejoicing, readers are encouraged to implement these mechanisms to welcome and sustain a BRAND-NEW DAY! This work intends to remind readers of those indigenous practices that have sustained many cultures in hopes of preparing them for the future that is to come. Ase'.

Characteristics of Conjure Expression

AIR flows

As you dance

Once they arrive

Move

Work with your body.

Cleanse your body.

Thank your body.

Listen to only what stirs you. Dance

Release the sorrow! Free your body! Free your mind!

Dance like you know the moves

Release that stress!

I can feel a BRAND-NEW DAY!

Release the weight of stiffness. Flow. REJOICE.

Move and be grateful.

Remember all you have overcome.

FIRE burns

Burn away your fear.

With lavender

and lemon grass

and chamomile

and mint

and rosemary- two tbsp.

Add some rose petals

and vervain

and cinnamon

and sage.

Light a candle!

Blow away your stress.

With mint

and lavender

and chamomile

and rose petals.

Light the herb!

Walk into the smoke. Can you feel the GLORY?

Breathe in 2

Hold 2

Breathe out 2

Look at the flick of the wick!

What is it telling you? Keep moving forward.

Light it up like you aren't afraid to get burned!

REJOICE!

I can feel a BRAND-NEW DAY!

Release the weight of care.

Blow and be grateful

Remember all you have burned away.

WATER washes

The water that cleanses and refreshes

Bathe in sea salt

and lavender

and peppermint

and chamomile

and jasmine

and hibiscus.

Let mama cleanse your soul. 1 or 3 or 5 or 7 times a week. Until you feel renewed.

Speak life into your water

Be glad that she knows who you are.

Sing songs and write letters about your near jubilee!

What are you praying for? Do the work

Let go of your past and embrace your future. Embrace your win.

Lay low and feel the vibrations.

What are you thankful for?

Let your pores pour!

Take a deep breath

Feel the weight of the past. Honor it. Release it.

Surrender to the water. Be fluid.

REJOICE!

I can feel a BRAND-NEW DAY!

Release the fear of drowning.

Know.

REJOICE.

Remember all you have washed away.

EARTH covers

Close your eyes. Breathe in. Breathe out.

What do you see?

REJOICE. REJOICE. Imagine Victory.

Stand strong. Plant your feet. Raise your hands above your head and be a column of light.

With one breath. One movement. One body.

Swan dive over.

Now do a forward fold.

Half lift.

Breathe.

Bend your knees.

Get into table top position

Cat

now

Cow

Swing your legs around.

Sit on your bottom. Now crisscross applesauce.

Breathe.

Place your hands on your knees. Ground yourself. Rotate. This way

Stop and find your center.

Lay flat on your back and put the soles of your feet on the mat. Sink.

Become one with the earth.

REJOICE!

I can feel a BRAND-NEW DAY!

Release the weight of your mind.

Go within

Harness your strength.

Remember how grounded you are.

SOMETHING YOU SHOULD KNOW

In all your work

And consider this

You

reap

what

you

sow.

So

sow

what

you

want

to

GROW!

Chapter 7
La Negrita Chronicles | Frania G. Romulus

Frania G. Romulus was born in Boston, MA. As a child Romulus loved to create, perform and act. It is no surprise that writing came so easily to her. She began playwriting in elementary school as a bright student in the Talented and Gifted program. As the years passed Romulus focused her artistic talent to strictly traveling and competing as a serious saxophonist in her high school music assemblies. She was reminded of her gift of writing while an undergrad at Clark University. She matriculated with a degree in Psychology and Performing Arts.

Romulus' work portrays her experiences as a woman of color at a predominantly white institution. Her raw emotional honesty, uncomfortable dialogue, and satirical style won the attention of Playfest then AS220, enabling her piece to be on production as well as earning her an artist residency.

Trendy euphemisms, allusions, modern references, and diverse casting help Romulus connect to today's audience. The artist uses her platform and voice to illustrate advocacy through art, addressing the difficult conflicts of race facing our country today.

Romulus explains, "Women of color are expected to be silenced, I demand my voice to be heard." Using comedy the playwright engages the audience as she weaves a powerful personal tale of a heroine surviving rape, racism and heartbreak.

The artist hopes that her art will leave an impression on others, and create the space for these difficult, yet necessary dialogues to formulate.

***

Frania Romulus' play La Negrita Chronicles is based loosely on events of her time at Clark University. Clark's motto is "categorizing is not something we do here" yet Frania found herself being categorized at every turn. Being multi-ethnic and proud, Romulus absolutely DESPISES being told by OTHERS how she should perceive herself! Frania's experiences at Clark were the first time she faced blatant discrimination. So, naturally, she wrote a comedic satire about it.

Her underlying message is such: love is not enough, love doesn't fix, and love doesn't solve every problem. Women of color are systematically oppressed and yet are expected to be "strong". To overcome obstacles of any kind, no matter the circumstance. And the fact of the matter is, women of color, are WOMEN, which means they are human. They do not possess any superhuman strength that makes them able to survive the impossible. Most literature on minorities is written through a white lens. A lens that does not hold any cultural authenticity, for what does a white man or woman know of a person of color's struggle? Her lens tells the reality of things: women of color usually have no happy ending. Her grandmother did not, her mother did not, she WILL not. She Will not. She will...not.

La Negrita Chronicles is a play in 4 acts with the airing time of approximately 50 minutes.

La Negrita Chronicles

Timeline

Scene I: Scandal

Scene II: B-U-D-D-Y

Scene III: I Make It Rain on These Hoes

Scene IV: Fight Club

Scene V: I Thought White Niggas Were Too Scared to Fuck Me...

Scene VI: Wrecking Ball: Army of Gays

Scene VII: Kissland

Scene VIII: I just want to have enough faith in the white race that one day I will find my non-Oppressor

Scene IX: The Coffee Shop (Since All Great Plays Seem to Have One)

Scene X: Witch Bitch

Scene XI: Trust Issues

Note: Scene headings are to be projected.

Characters

LA NEGRITA – *Afro- Caribbean*

MACHINE GUN KIKI – *Afro-Caribbean, Latina, Creole, or African American*

BOUKIE – *Woman of color*

BUDDY JUNIOR, JR. – *White male*

ESAU – Young *Black male, addicted to retail*

FRANKIE – *Aryan looking white nigga*

FLAMING FILIPPE – *Glamorous gay*

NURSE RATCHET – *Nurse dressed in drag*

MO'NICA VANE – *Indigenous or white-presenting Latina*

Scene I: Scandal

(*Security guard in beginning scene played by Frankie*)

LA NEGRITA

Hi, I'm LA NEGRITA, this is my story, this is my song. Welcome to my world of **scandal** and oppression. I was on my way to be a kind, gentle and **obedient** Negress, until I got a phone call from my best friend MACHINE GUN KIKI. She requested I immediately come to her rescue at the Institution of Achievement for Colored Ritards. She's always going off complaining about white people this, white people that. Trying to disrupt the order of things. But this is the circle of life. This is social structure. There's no such thing as social mobility, or racial mobility! So I know my place in society, it's the back of the bus for me! That's how I got here! Colored folks ain't got no cars. It's okay though, white people aren't that bad...(*Whispers to audience.*) Just don't tell MACHINE GUN KIKI I said that!

KIKI

(*Whispers in a strained voice.*) La Negrita.

LA NEGRITA

Yes menina?

KIKI

Hold my hand.

LA NEGRITA

But menina, how am I to hold your hand?

KIKI

(*KIKI looks down at her wrists to see that they are bandaged and hand-cuffed to the bed. Security guard surrounds her.*)

LA NEGRITA

Menina, your hands.

KIKI

(*Getting upset.*) THEY DID THIS TO ME!!!!!!

LA NEGRITA

Who did this to you menina? (*Rushes to friend, on knees, holds on to the one free finger that has escaped the bandage.*)

KIKI

Who do you think?

LA NEGRITA

Yo no se menina.

KIKI

(*Says to audience.*) It was the whhhhhites! The same people responsible for tricking blacks into thinking they are helping when in reality they started it all. They are arrogant and carry privileges only they understand. Jungle Fever, oppression. They condemn us. They kiss their children on the lips, walk them on leashes, and leave them alone in an empty room: A cold bassinet. They ignore their cries and instead train them like puppies to "self soothe"; a ritual foreign and paradoxical to us. Creating Twitter accounts for their unborn children.

Beat.

They put alien objects like cucumbers, broccoli, carrots, tulips, kale chips and cinnamon sticks in their water to drink. What are they, fuckin wood nymphs?

Beat.

Turn 18, kick you out the house.

Beat.

White America got everything and some. They **love** America too much and **always** name their children 'Junior' **AND ALWAYS CALL EACH OTHER BUDDY!!!** (*Pause.*) White athletes snort Adderall in their locker rooms! Unprotected sex... Leaving behind their iPads at the gym. Trips to exotic places on Spring break...

Beat.

Use measuring cups when they're cooking... The Cups Song. Solo cups. **DIVA** cups.

Beat.

Changing the color of their hair to match the rainbow, like we change the textures of our weaves. Touching ethnic hair... All white people look the same. Their blonde hair blends with their translucent, never-been-touched-by-the-sun, Edward Cullen skin. Don't get too close, or our make-up will stain their pale, pasty faces. White people be the **devil**. White people got me **FUCKED UP.** They be the bane of my existence.

Beat.

White people do not bathe regularly. Lice... White people have hair they can wash every day, but often don't condition. They shampoo, rinse, repeat. (*Pause. Awkward silence.*) They have this hair, that just grows overnight and changes texture with length. One minute it's all short and straight, the next it grows all long and curly.

Beat.

White people CRAY—Pools in their backyard. White people wear swimming caps to the swimming pool, making the oldies look like a wrinkly penis wearing a condom.

Beat.

I don't know anyone whose favorite color is white! I don't know anyone who likes white chocolate! They love hockey too much. Bird watching...white people have time for that. White people eat sandwiches and milk for breakfast, dinner AND lunch. Runny eggs. Bloody meats.

Beat.

White people want to be ethnic. They tan till they skin be leathery, use Botox so they won't age. Kylie Jenner's lips. Black don't crack! Dreading their hair.

Beat.

They kiss their pets on the lips...hell, they'll do ANYTHING to a damn pet! Shit, they'll MARRY their damn pet! Wear their pets in harnesses across they chests like they do to they own damn childrun. Doggy bag. Dead give-away.

Beat.

White people have real snacks in their household, not just arroz. All the things they do, But **I** is the one sent to this here Cuckoo's Nest...

LA NEGRITA

Oh God! #BigSean. What have the whites done this time??!!

KIKI

Oppress me of course. What else are they good at besides slavery?

LA NEGRITA

Menina, what did they do to you??!!

KIKI

They slit my wrists. Made me write "nigger" in blood a thousand times. Off the wall #MichealJackson. Then had the AUDACITY to send ME to a MENTAL WARD!!! (*Starts spazzing the fuck off. Trying to remove the chains to no avail. Security guard snicker.*)

LA NEGRITA

(*Says to audience.*) Menina, whites are cruel, bitter and oppressive by nature. It is in their genetic make-up. But the whites must be provoked. What did you do? Did you make eye contact without their permission??!!

KIKI

After they made me write "nigger" in blood a thousand times, they then forced me to write a paper about how great it is to be white. (*Turns to audience.*) My paper was short, like the white man's dick. (*Spits out glaring at security guards.*)

LA NEGRITA

How did this begin?

KIKI

(*Says under breath.*) I choked a white bitch.

LA NEGRITA

KIKI!!! (*Gasps.*)

KIKI

She called me a "nigger"! They straight trying to regulate a regulator!

LA NEGRITA

(*Says to audience.*) Menina, that is what we are! Nothing MORE, nothing LESS! White is right! It even rhymes, so I know that statement is factual!

Beat.

White people are our savior. They are our supremacists. We are below them in every shape, way and form. To be pasty, pale, and featureless is to be beautiful. To be flat chested is to be a queen. To have a poncho-wearing white girl ass (*looks back at it*) is the only thing that will save us!

KIKI

(*Directed to audience.*) poncho wearin titty lackin blonde ass pussy bitch. I'm at the point where I don't even dislike it. bitches like that make bitches like us look better, so let 'em starve till they hipbones pop, they doin us a favor.

Beat.

White girls are like cardboards...no ass or titties. For the few that have asses, they mixed. The ones with titties either stuff they bra or its saggy. LONG TITTY NO NIPPLE BITCH!

Beat.

White girls only have two outfit choices. Yoga pants, Uggs and a Northface jacket in the winter...and a skimpy tank top with the same short shorts they have worn since the summer of our lives. (*Shakes her head at LA NEGRITA who is dressed exactly as such.*)

LA NEGRITA

KIKI, why couldn't you just be grateful enough that the whites let us go to college. We started from the bottom now we hea. We started from the bottom, now my whole fuckin team hea.

KIKI

Bitch, where??!! Where is we???!! We started at the bottom... WE STILL AT THE FUCKIN BOTTOM!!!!!!!!!!!!!!! College, menina? You call this college? Nigga, I'm not even allowed in the lunch line!

Beat.

This ain't college menina, this is flight school!

LA NEGRITA

I'm tired of yo ratchet ass, why you gotta stir up trouble??!!

KIKI

Stir up trouble? Bitch, a white nigga calls me a "nigger". So I call her one back. Next thing I know I'm in a headlock being buttfucked by the police. Slittin mah wrists. Making me write a short dick "nigger" essays in mah blood. So I'm mad and start tweeting and bleeding on my IPHONE talking about I wanna go to a shooting range. Next thing I know the fucking president of the Kim Kanye Kevin University wanna come at me talking about my Creole ass poses as a

THREAT to the INSTITUTION OF WHITENESS. Talking about Imma shoot up the school.

LA NEGRITA

And take on the whites? That's crazy! It's never been done!

KIKI

My sentiments exactly my Negress friend.

Beat.

White niggas be the only niggas crazy enough to shoot up a school and shit! With black niggas, they just shoot you "Bang, bang" you dead. But no, white niggas got all kinds of fucked up shit wrong with them. Going to elementary schools killing babies. Going to the movies, killing couples. Taking niggas hostage, torturing them. Cutting their limbs. Eating it. Masturbating on dead bodies... (*Looks at the nigga rollin up in a hospital bed.*)

Beat.

Yo Negrita, is that your brother?

LA NEGRITA

ESAU!?

JEROME

Belky?!

LA NEGRITA

What are you doing here??

ESAU

(*Says to audience.*) I've been oppressed!

KIKI

#same. What the whites do to you?

ESAU

Valentine's Day... chillin. In the Bean with my niggas and shit. We poppin bottles. Poppin pussy. I was on these white bitches like Seal nigga. So this white nigga approached me. I says, "Oh that was yo girl? I thought I recognized her." To which he responded, "nigger". So I choked that nigga! Why do these white niggas think they can ball, dance, jump, fight, fuck, RAP. THEY AINT SHIT NIGGA!

KIKI

You know what? FUCK Seal Nigga! What the fuck he talking about, "You became my light on the dark side of me..." Kiss by a Rose type shit...Nigga EVERY SIDE OF YOU IS DARK! YOU IS BLACK AS **ALL** HELL!!!

LA NEGRITA

They named him "Seal" because he be black as ALL hell.

ESAU

(*Starts "cheffin"- dance move.*) All these snow bunnies want me cuz they got that BDV!

LA NEGRITA

BDV?

ESAU

Black Dick Vision!

KIKI

You heard what they did to my boy Jose right?

ESAU

No bro, que paso!?

KIKI

They Trayvon-ed his ass!

ESAU

(*Gasps.*)

LN

"They"?

KIKI

White people La Negrita! When will you get that through that nappy haired head of yours! He had a fucking bag of **M&Ms and a bottle of Coco Rico, and they straight SHOT that nigga.**

Beat.

The police just be shooting EVERYBODY!

ESAU

He wasn't ready! Hold up, Woah derrr! #BigSean. MONICA VANE?! (*VANE is being rolled in a stretcher.*)

LA NEGRITA / KIKI

Manita?! / Menina?

VANE

I heard bands so I wanted to dance.

LA NEGRITA

Manita, what are you doing here? You are all tied up!

KIKI

No shit Einstein.

VANE / ESAU

KIKI, what are doing here? / VANE, what are you doing here?

VANE

I've been oppressed!

KIKI

Haven't we all, my friend.

LA NEGRITA

What happened to you?

VANE

I was at the movie theatre, With my date. Trying to live my life to the fullest and have a Black Movie Tuesday.

KIKI

With your date?

VANE

My date! I met him on Blackpeoplemeet.com. He is kind, gentle and colored and has all the breaks to handle my curves girl! (*Makes car breaking gesture.*)

KIKI

Oh yes, hear here.

VANE

So, we go to the snack line first, trying to get snacks. And this nigga talking about the theatre closing soon, who wants free popcorn? This white devil LOOKS ME RIGHT IN THE EYES, and only gives a bag of popcorn to my date.

VANE

But he a colored!

LA NEGRITA

That bastard.

VANE

It gets worse. I go to line and before I could even open my full-lipped mouth, this whitey whips out a quick, "We don't air Black movies here". And I say, "Cool, I didn't want to watch Django anyways." Next thing I know I was AMBUSHED by the police. They took their clubs and beat me to no avail. If that wasn't enough, they sent their police dogs after us. They could smell the nigger in my date's blood and they attacked him as well.

LA NEGRITA

Whaaaaaaaaaaaaaaaaaaaat.

VANE

(Flares eyes at LA NEGRITA.) Are you surprised? White people may be many things. But kind or gentle they are not.

KIKI

And what bullshit reason did they give you?

VANE

I was dressed like a gypsy *(Points to flowy Grecian dress.)* and they fuckin attacked me.

KIKI

But you look like Aphrodite, reincarnated, and brought to earth to show these hip-poppin, toilet-cloggin, Snooki-works-out-too-much bitches, what real women are actually supposed to look like! #Dove

VANE

Like, what the fuck. Biologically, women that look like us, With bodies like ours, are supposed to be favored! But no, instead they condemn us. They ruin our interracial dates, and instead send dogs to attack me.

LA NEGRITA

Why? But why manita? Why do these people do such things?

VANE

Because this isn't fuckin Oz, La Negrita. This is a Cole fuckin world, no snuggie. They beat me, sent me here, and said under the circumstances I should understand.

ESAU

What circumstances?

VANE

The fact there was a shooting at another movie theatre.

LA NEGRITA

And who was responsible for that shooting?

VANE

The whites of course!

Beat.

When the police officer was done beating me, he said I have the perfect body, for the wrong century.

Beat.

Whatever, I'm too hot.com for these bitches anyways. (*Does Amazonian warrior scream, throws signs in the air, and falls backward onto hospital bed.*)

(*Boukie is wheeled in by a stretcher as well and placed on hospital bed, by guards.*)

KIKI / LA NEGRITA

BOUKIE! / BOO!

BOUKIE

(*Looks around.*) MACHINE GUN KIKI? ESAU? VANE!? QUE, QUE? TOMA REGGAETON!!!

VANE

Manita, what are you doing here?

BOUKIE

What are y'all doing here??

ESAU

It has been a night of oppression.

LA NEGRITA

Boo, what happened?

BOUKIE

Speedin' #Omarion

ESAU

Well, manita, how fast were you going?

BOUKIE

You know. Going 26 in a 25 mile per hour lane.

LA NEGRITA

One mile above the speed limit?!?!

KIKI

(Sarcastically.) Good job, menina, you can count.

BOUKIE

Can't I just tell niggas I wasn't speeding? I was auditioning for a Fast and Furious movie? (*kisses helmet and raises it to the sky*) R.I.P. Paul Walker.

(*extended silence. Cast looks at her.*)

BOUKIE

Too soon?

KIKI

(*Changes subject.*) Bitch, this is 2015! You think they ever let no coloreds grace a TV screen?

LA NEGRITA

What about the Boondocks?

KIKI

You dumb bitch, that's a cartoon!

(*FLAMING FILIPPE gets wheeled in.*)

BOUKIE

Filippe?!?!

FLAMING FILIPPE

(*Looks at them one by one.*) LA NEGRITA? ESAU? MACHINE GUN KIKI? VANE? BOUKIE? What are y'all doing here?

VANE

Us?

Beat.

What are **you** doing here?!?!

FLAMING FILIPPE

Honey **look** at me. (*Cast looks at him adorned in pink princess tiara, pink nails, and pink fur coat.*)

Beat.

Honey, I just been Oscar Wilded.

LA NEGRITA

I don't get it. White people **can't** bet that bad. I mean, they have it all, nice cars, names you can pronounce. Summers of their lives. Dinners at restaurants e'ry night. They never face discrimination. they don't have clingy friends that don't pick up on social cues...

FLAMING FILIPPE

White people are irrelevant La Negrita! They wear shorts and flip flops to shovel during Juno for heaven's fuck! White people drink coffee, no milk, no honey #Rupi...They get traumatized over divorce, read their younger siblings bedtime stories, get dates to dances, can't pronounce anything not English, say your name wrong...

Beat.

They insist you have a fat ass no matter how mediocre the ass is. They partake in YOLO sports such as underwater kisses; jogging during blizzards. White people **want** to die. It's their white guilt! They want to experience a struggle so they sabotage their own inherent advantages...

Beat.

They hold onto limbs that they need to amputate... They name their kids after states...Adopt babies from Africa...White people do not cook and aren't always there when you call, but are **always** on time...

Beat.

White people go through soda like its water... Polar Beverages.

Beat.

White people have nice cars, which they don't utilize if a destination is in walking distance. They drop $200 to buy drugs, when they could just be buying weave...White people love hockey **too much**! I just don't get it.

(*NURSE RATCHET enters.*)

NURSE RATCHET

Well hello. Welcome to the Institute of Achievement for Colored—Retards. My name is Nurse Ratchet, pronounced Ratchet, as in (*Points to member of audience.)* "Fix yo weave! You look Ratchet". And it seems as though 1. *(Points at KIKI.)* 2. *(Points at ESAU.)* 3. *(Points at VANE.)* 4. *(Points at BOUKIE.)* 5. *(Points at FLAMING FILIPPE.)* ...have flown over the cuckoo's nest. *(Starts hysterically laughing squeezing syringe.)* Now face down, ass up, **shawty!** I'll be yo medicine this evening.

(ESAU and VANE look to each other terrified. KIKI starts banging her fists against the bed angrily, never breaking eye contact with LA NEGRITA.)

LA NEGRITA

Okay, this is just not fair. I ain't Winona Ryder, you ain't Angelina Jolie.

KIKI

(Begins blood curdling screams.)

VANE

(Looks to LA NEGRITA.) Girl, you just been interrupted.

LA NEGRITA

What are you going to do? What are you all going to do?!

VANE

Escape of course!

NURSE RATCHET

Nigga, ain't NOBODY got time for that. Y'all will be lucky if you even get discharged.

Beat.

Now hurry it along Negress, visiting hours are just about over. *(Snaps finger.)* We'll have a security guard escort you out.

(FRANKIE approaches LA NEGRITA and escorts her off stage.)

BLACKOUT.

Scene II: B-U-D-D-Y

LA NEGRITA

You know what they say about white boys? Well it's not true. Well, for BUDDY, JR. at least! Yeah, he's white. You might have thought my visit with my fam and friends earlier at the Institute of Achievement for Colored Retards would deter me from the whites, but what can I say? They ain't done me no harm! See no evil, hear no evil, speak no evil?

(*Track and field of KKK University. BUDDY is jogging towards LA NEGRITA. She jogs in nothing but a bright pink sports bra, and spanks. Light Rain. Slight work.*)

BUDDY

(*Pulls out LA NEGRITA's headphones. Grabs her and swirls her about.*) Hi baby. (*He flashes her a beautiful smile.*)

LA NEGRITA

BUDDY (*Smiles. Kisses him.*) Coach making you run sprints?

BUDDY

(*Holds her hand. They start walking.*) No baby. Do you know nothing about hockey?

LA NEGRITA

No.

BEAT.

I'm not white, remember? (*Says sadly, under breath.*)

BUDDY

It's okay babe. (*Runs hands through hair.*) We can work on that.

LA NEGRITA

So, what are you doing here? (*Starts stretching.*)

BUDDY

I dunno babe. You just been running through my mind all day, I thought I'd catch up to you. (*Grins.*)

LA NEGRITA

HAHA.

BUDDY

Stop babe. (*Kisses her. Kisses hand. Places his hand in hers.* **Hands** *her his jacket.*)

LA NEGRITA

Such a gentleman, I appreciate the sentiment

Beat.

(*Hands him back jacket.*) But it's humid.

BUDDY

(*Looks up at rain. Then towards field. Angrily looks at team at practice*) Take it babe. (*Wraps her in his jacket. It engulfs her tiny, yet curvy frame.*) They're looking at you.

LA NEGRITA

Who? (*Takes sip of water bottle.*)

BUDDY

The fuckin' team.

LA NEGRITA

Oh? (*Laughs.*) Why?

BUDDY

(*Sounds embarrassed. As if her being sexy is something embarrassing.*) Cuz—you're sexy. (*Looks away.*)

LA NEGRITA

(*Laughs.*) Well sorry!

BUDDY

It's okay. I guess it's not your fault you're sexy. I just—I don't want anyone looking at what's mine.

LA NEGRITA

What's yours?

BUDDY

Do you trust me?

LA NEGRITA

Excuse me?

BUDDY

Do I make you feel safe?

LA NEGRITA

(*Looks at whhhhhhite man puzzled.*)

BUDDY

Babe, have you given me any consideration? Like this has been going on for months now. I just wanna know, that you're mine, and only mine. I wanna know, that I'm not sharing you with anybody else.

LA NEGRITA

Wait...So let me get this politically correct. You're allowed to be with other girls, but I can't see other guys?

BUDDY

Yeah! Exactly! (*Seems excited.*)

LA NEGRITA

Well, that doesn't seem that fair...

BUDDY

It's called an "open relationship..."

LA NEGRITA

If it was an open relationship, that would mean I would be allowed any man I please. If it was open that would mean you would want your friends to know. Like screw the team. Y'all are D3!

Beat.

Are you ashamed of me?

Beat.

What's wrong with me?

BUDDY

(*Looks wounded. Lowers voice.*) Is that what you think Nina?

Beat.

You think I'm ashamed?

LA NEGRITA

(*Eyes water. Turns from him.*) Yo no se. (*Whispers.*) What do you want me to think?

BUDDY

That I really like you. I enjoy spending time with you. I like you a lot. I'm just trying to protect you. The things the team says about you...

LA NEGRITA

I don't care BUDDY JUNIOR, JR.! I don't care what people say about me! And until you don't care either, no BUDDY JUNIOR, JR.- I won't be in a stupid "open relationship" with you. (*Starts jogging off.*)

BUDDY

(*Runs after her.*) Babe, ugh. Come back!

Beat.

It's not that. It's uncomfortable, okay? I'm tired of hearing my teammates talking in the locker room about how bad they fucking want to bone you. Calling you the Goddess of the Kneller, Voluptuous Vixen of the Dickman. Babe, you are Proctor of my Life, can't you see that! (*Grabs her into a lip-locking kiss.*)

LA NEGRITA

I can't.

BUDDY

C'mon. (*Holds her hand. Zips up his jacket around her.*)

LA NEGRITA

I have to go.

BUDDY

You have to go with me.

LA NEGRITA

I can't.

BUDDY

With me.

(*Big pause, she thinks about it, thinks about it more, he slaps her booty, takes her hand, they go.*)

BLACKOUT.

Scene III: I Make it Rain on These Hoes

(Moments later. Dorm room. On BUDDY's bed. BUDDY lights up a blunt. They are post coital. "Marijuana" by Kid Cudi plays in the background.)

BUDDY

3 minutes, my new record!

Beat.

(After moments of looking at LA NEGRITA.) You're mine right?

LA NEGRITA

Can I call you Junior?

⫽BUDDY

Why?

LA NEGRITA

(Looks down at Buddy's...JUNIOR. There's a pause.) Why do white people do drugs?

BUDDY

Because it enhances our sexual experience *and performance. (Puts out blunt, and kisses her instead.)* Because our lives are filled with apathy and boredom, and we need something to fill the void.

LA NEGRITA

What the hell? Why don't you like get a job.

BUDDY

Job? White people don't **have** to do that shit.

Beat.

But me? I want to be a mayor someday. Just like my dad *(beams.)*

LA NEGRITA

Sometimes when I see white people my age working, I think to myself. Why you working? I know your parents give you money. But, I shouldn't think that way. I'm a bad person.

BUDDY

You're not a bad person babe. You're just black. And we're going to work on that, okay babe? *(Laughs.)*

(Puts mango in his mouth. Draws a map of the world with its pulp on LA NEGRITA.)

  Beat.

Baby. *(Whispers.)*

LA NEGRITA

Mmmmmm.

BUDDY

Where is your family from?

LA NEGRITA

New York.

BUDDY

(Places finger on LA NEGRITA's lips to silence her.) No, where are they REALLY from?

LA NEGRITA

Buddy—Washington Heights...New York.

BUDDY

Babyyyyy, you can tell me! It's okay. I love this shit. I just want to know which part of Africa you're really from. Ghana, Nigeria, the Nile?

LA NEGRITA

Buddy, I'm Dominican.

BUDDY

Where's that? (*LA NEGRITA gives him dumb look.*) Such a lovely sound. (*Looks outside window.*)

Beat.

It's still raining out.

LA NEGRITA

Pardon?

BUDDY

The rain, it's beautiful. It's beautiful.

BEAT

It's—it's a lovely sound. (*Smiles at her, kisses her gently again.*)

Beat.

So is this a yes?

LA NEGRITA

What?

BUDDY

Will you be mine?

LA NEGRITA

I don't know.

BUDDY

(*Distracted by the rain.*) I love the rain.

BEAT

I love running in the rain. I love making **love** in the rain (*Turns to face her.*) The sound of rain is almost as beautiful as your face. (*Kisses LA NEGRITA's forehead.*) I love the rain, (*Squeezes her hand.*) and I think I just might love you. (*Smiles.*)

LA NEGRITA

(*Gets up abruptly. Starts fishing for clothes.*)

BUDDY

What's wrong? For the love of fuck, where are you going?

LA NEGRITA

(*Looks up at him.*) I'm leaving Buddy, what do you think?

BUDDY

What did I say? (*Pause, she looks at him*). Baby, **please** be mine? You are oh so beautiful. With your mocha skin, expressive hair. Everything about you is exotic.

LA NEGRITA

(*Looks up at him.*) And what pray tell, exactly, is that supposed to mean?

BUDDY

I ask you to be my girl. I tell you that I love you, I make LOVE to you...what the fuck is that? Is that not action enough for you?

LA NEGRITA

This was a mistake.

BUDDY

Why?

LA NEGRITA

One of your girls. Buddy Jr., you asked me to be **one** of your girls. What is this whole open relationship bullshit? What does it consist of? Are you like a damn Mormon? Will I have sister wives? Can you just not choose one, so you gotta catch them all? #Pokemon

 BUDDY

(*Raises eyebrows. Says quietly.*) I said that I love you.

 LA NEGRITA

You said you "think" that you love me.

 BUDDY

I'm working on it.

 LA NEGRITA

You're **always** "working on it." Let me know when you're done "working on it".

(*She exits.*)

BLACKOUT.

Scene IV: FIGHT CLUB

(Swalla by Jeremih and Nicki Minaj play in the background of LA NEGRITA's dorm room.)

BOUKIE

C'mon Negrita. Let's go out tonight.

LA NEGRITA

I dunno Boukie. I just...I don't want to get him mad.

BOUKIE

PLEASE don't tell me you're talking about that D1 wanna be Buddy Jr. and his "open relationships."

Beat.

Everything about him is stupid. His stupid relationships. Even his name is stupid.

LA NEGRITA

Come now, menina. Be nice, that's my man.

BOUKIE

Your man menina? I don't see the ring. He doesn't even ACKNOWLEDGE your presence in public, and he's gonna tell you where, and when you can go out?

LA NEGRITA

I dunno. He just has a funny way of showing it.

BOUKIE

Of showing what?

LA NEGRITA

That he loves me...

BOUKIE

Funny, all right. You are too Fifty Shades of Sexy to be wasting yo time with a lame. You best get with a REAL nigga like me!

LA NEGRITA

Boukie, you're a girl. I just...I don't play on that team.

BOUKIE

Well, you gon learn tuhday!

LA NEGRITA

I'm a basketball wife...

BOUKIE

Girl, you are a HOCKEY HOE!

(They go from the dorm to the cab. From the cab to the club. From the windows to the wall, to the sweat drip down my balls. All these females crawl. Ohhhhh skeet skeet mothafucka, oh skeet skeet!)

BOUKIE

(Slurring words, slurring her body. Feelin herself.) I am feelin MAHSELF!

LA NEGRITA

I know girl, I am feeling, looking, smelling like a million bucks!

BOUKIE

Bitch, you looking bad like a stack of money!

LA NEGRITA

Thanks girl. Pretty on fleek!

BOUKIE

Turnt up! *(Squints eyes across the dance floor.)* But yo, is that yo man?

LA NEGRITA

Girl, you know I have no man when we in public. (*Bursts into fits of laughter.*)

BOUKIE

Damn, that sucks bro.

LA NEGRITA

But he is looking 50 Shades of Dapper tonight. (*Looks at him, licks lips.*)

(*Tipsy, LA NEGRITA tiptoes over to BUDDY, covering his eyes with her hands.*)

LA NEGRITA

Guess who? (*FRANKIE stares at LA NEGRITA. Music spins.*)

BUDDY

(*Smiles, as he begins to open his eyes. When he opens his eyes, his excitement soon turns to anger.*)

FRANKIE

Yo, Buddy Jr., you know this hoe?!

BUDDY

Hell no, I don't know this here colored hoe. I do not fornicate with those of colors!

FRANKIE

Good thing man! (*Takes sip of handle.*) Fuck colored bitches!

BUDDY and FRANKIE

Yeah, fuck colored bitches!

FRANKIE

But not literally doe! Yeah, you know them bitches got all types of black diseases. Like AIDS and syphilis cuz they be fuckin monkeys.

LA NEGRITA

But I'm Latina. And Christopher Columbus along with his clan of filthy Europeans came to my country centuries ago and brought his damn STDS. Cuz THIS pussy good!!!

BOUKIE

Here, here! (*Raises glass.*)

BUDDY

That don't matter! (*Shoves her. Before she knows it, FRANKIE is shoving her too.*)

FRANKIE

Are they real? (*Eyes her chest. Eyes her eyes. Reaches out his hands to grab them.*)

Beat.

Black people violate traditional White values such as hard-work and independence.

Beat.

The failure of Blacks to progress results from their unwillingness to work hard enough.

Beat.

Blacks are demanding **too** much **too** fast.

Beat.

(*FRANKIE AND BUDDY toast.*)

Beat.

And lastly— (*Directed to LA NEGRITA.*) Blacks have gotten **MORE** than they deserve... (*Shoves BOUKIE.*) Faggot.

BOUKIE

I'm not a faggot! (*Shoves FRANKIE back.*) Racist!

FRANKIE

Hey! Irish, Italian, and many other minorities overcame prejudice and worked their way up. Blacks should do the same!

(*LUKE steps in. FRANKIE and LUKE begin to brawl. BOUKIE attempts to break up fight. Actors run off on all opposite directions of stage.*)

BLACKOUT.

Scene V: I Thought White Niggas Were Too Scared to Fuck Me

LA NEGRITA

(*Hears someone come into the bathroom.*) Boukie?

BUDDY

Ohhhhhhhh, we slapping coochies now? Feeling better now? Gucci sweater now?

LA NEGRITA

(*Yelling.*) BUDDY, GET THE HELL OUT!

BUDDY

Or what? (*Grins evilly.*)

LA NEGRITA

Buddy, what happened to you? What is **wrong** with you?

BUDDY

What's wrong with me?

LA NEGRITA

You're never like this!

BUDDY

Well, I'm drunk! (*Downs some more liquor.*)

LA NEGRITA

Stop it!

BUDDY

And, I'm pissed off you know. How DARE you walk out on me?!

LA NEGRITA

I—I'll be your girl! It will only be you. Even with you acting like this.

BUDDY

Oh, now you want me!

LA NEGRITA

Please—I do! I still want to be with you.

BUDDY

I tell you I love you, that I want to be with you, and then you just leave me? Nobody LEAVES me! I am BUDDY JUNIOR, JR.! (*Beats chest.*)

LA NEGRITA

I want to be with you, I do.

Beat.

I want for us to truly be together.

BUDDY / LA NEGRITA

It's too late. / I think I love you too.

BUDDY

Well, I don't love you anymore.

LA NEGRITA

But you told me you loved me just two scenes ago...

BUDDY

Bitch, I don't want you!

LA NEGRITA

We can still be together—

BUDDY

Not with you dressed like THIS. You know I HATE when you dress like a **slut**. You know it makes me mad.

LA NEGRITA

Please, not like this!

BUDDY

(Ripping off her skirt.) Listening to the team talk about how badly they want fuck you—well they won't want you after I'm through!

LA NEGRITA

Buddy, give me the bottle! *(LA NEGRITA tries to grab bottle.)*

BUDDY

This bottle? *(Finishes entire bottle and uses it to hit LA NEGRITA over the head. Bottle breaks. Blood is everywhere, matting her weave. "Put You in a Room" by Nicki Minaj starts to play in background.)*

BLACKOUT.

Scene VI: Wrecking Ball: ARMY OF GAYS!

(BOUKIE knocks frantically on FLAMING FILIPPE'S door.)

FLAMING FILIPPE

Come in!!! *(FLAMING FILIPPE sits at his crown with a facemask of Vivaporu and semen. He is adorned in a fur coat and princess tiara on his head.)*

(BOUKIE enters.)

FLAMING FILIPPE

Boukie! My favorite bisexual friend! Sit, sit! *(Leads friend to seat.)*

Beat.

You're just in time for my tea party!!! *(Pours BOUKIE a cup.)*

BOUKIE

Fine china. *(Sings in tune reminiscent to Chris Brown's smash hit.)*

FLAMING FILIPPE

I know!

Beat.

So what brings you here this fine evening? Honey boo boo, you look BEAT.

BOUKIE

Flamer, would you mind if I crash here tonight?

FLAMING FILIPPE

Of course, Boo, I LOVE sleepovers!! *(Getting excited and swirling about.)*

Beat.

Will La Negrita be joining us?

(BOUKIE spits out her tea.)

FLAMING FILIPPE

Speaking of which, I haven't seen that little nappy headed ray of sunshine in quite some time!

Beat.

Now tell me, how is she?

BOUKIE

A whore.

FLAMING FILIPPE

BOUKIE! *(Admonishes friend.)* Now don't you **dare** speak of my dearest friend is such a way! *(Shrieks.)*

(Someone will knock at door.)

FLAMING FILIPPE

Coming! *(Says to BOUKIE.)* Oh, I am OH so popular!

(Enters ESAU.)

BOUKIE

What's up Esau. *(Esau goes over kisses Boukie on cheek. FLAMING comes towards ESAU to kiss him as well.)*

ESAU

No homo dawg. *(Says to HOMO.)*

FLAMING FILIPPE

Fine. What is it with 'you people' and homophobia?

Beat.

Tea?

ESAU

Nah. I'm good.

BOUKIE

You sure you really good?

ESAU

Nah. Actually BOUKIE, have you seen LA NEGRITA?

BOUKIE

Only in the evening.

ESAU

What's that supposed to mean?

BOUKIE

ESAU, yo sister is a thot.

ESAU

Hey, don't talk about her like that!

FLAMING FILIPPE

Told you. Not nice. (*points finger at Boukie.*)

BOUKIE

Yo Flamer, do you know why I'm here?! LA NEGRITA turned our fuckin apartment into a fuckin brothel! Last night I caught her fucking coach!

ESAU

My sister would never! (*Getting defensive.*)

(*There is a knock on the door. LA NEGRITA stumbles into friend's home drunk.*)

BOUKIE

Ask her.

LA NEGRITA

It's a party, it's a party, it's a party!!

BOUKIE

La Negrita, where have you been? I haven't seen you since Fight Club. And that was about a week ago, week ago.

LA NEGRITA

Ugh Boukie, I hate when you stay keeping tabs on me. You're acting like you and I are a couple. God Boukie, **stawp! Stawp** being so in love with me!

BOUKIE

(*Says quietly, disappointed and wounded.*) You're drunk.

LA NEGRITA

You all want it. You, and Buddy, the team, coach. YOU ALL WANT ME!!!

ESAU

Hey, that's gross La Negrita, don't talk like that!

BOUKIE

La Negrita, you are drunk. On a Tuesday...

LA NEGRITA

The club's goin up, on a Tuesday—

ESAU

—Yo, I heard you're a thot. You need to stop fucking them white niggas. I'm telling mom.

LA NEGRITA

NO! I'm not That Hoe Over There. (*Reaches to grab ESAU, but stumbles over drunk in her stupor.*)

FLAMING FILIPPE

Girl, you sloppy. You look like a page ripped right out of Ratchet Jones' Diary! (*Shrieking with laughter at LA NEGRITA.*)

ESAU

Yo, I can't stay here and watch you act like this. I'm gonna chill with Kiki.

Beat.

Take care of her? (*Looks at friends.*)

BOUKIE & FLAMING FELIPPE

Of course.

ESAU

(*Towards LA NEGRITA.*) You need to do better.

LA NEGRITA

ESAU! (*Reaches to touch him.*)

ESAU

Don't touch me!

Beat.

(*Venomously.*) Hoe. (*Exits.*)

BOUKIE

What the fuck is wrong with you?!

LA NEGRITA

I'm just—I'm just tired. It's all— (*Says more quietly. Trying to center herself, trying to get the room to stop spinning.*)

FLAMING FILIPPE

Of course you're tired mi Negress. Cucumber Sandwich? (*Offers LA NEGRITA cucumber sandwich. FLAMING FILIPPE takes a bite.*)

Beat.

Whoring around is HUNGRY work!

LA NEGRITA

No. I'm just tired. BUDDY—

BOUKIE

No, La Negrita! Enough with the niggas man. Do you have any other selection in your vocabulary. Any other choice of topic. Like any— **a-n-y-t-h-i-n-g.** All you do is talk about these damn niggas whom you know perfectly well don't waste they precious **privileged** time talking 'bout you. I **warned** you!!

LA NEGRITA

BOO—

BOUKIE

—no please, don't even start. You're always fucking complaining. I'm really fucking tired of all **your** fucking complaining!

Beat.

Everybody's always complaining about their fucking relationships, something I know absolutely nothing about. It only reminds me of how lonely I am. Of how "alone", is all I know. (*looks angrily*) So here you are complaining about another stallion member of the hockey team wanting to fuck you, and you're complaining? Like what the fuck, at least you have a man who wants you, MEN who want you. The whole fucking team is always talking about you.

LA NEGRITA

Shut up Boukie.

BOUKIE

They say, "You cannot be lonely if you like the person you're alone with."
But... (*Starts to cry.*) That's a lie. I love myself. I truly, really do. But that
doesn't change the fact that I get lonely. That I want a person to love, a
person to love me too.

LA NEGRITA

Buddy doesn't want me. Nobody wants me. All he wanted was a 'open'
fucking relationship. Probably just so he could use me, and share me with
the whole fucking team.

FLAMING FILIPPE

Yo, why all these niggas be in open relationships, and I can't even get in **one**
relationship? It's fucking wack. Like fuck all these open ass relationships.
Just date us. Ugh. Just like...whose cock do I have to suck around here to
get a ring on my finger? (*Wiggles fingers.*) Or at least find someone who
wants me to suck theirs. Like am I not even good enough to be receptacle
to your cum?

BOUKIE

(*Looks up at FLAMING FILIPPE.*) And what's the point of being this
beautiful, if I'm always alone?—What-s the... what's the **point!?**

Beat.

Isn't it sad to be this beautiful but so unhappy?

FLAMING FILIPPE

Hear hear. (*Brings out pink handkerchief to wipe his tears.*)

(*LA NEGRITA goes over to console friend.*)

LA NEGRITA

Boukie, the reason you haven't found anyone isn't because you're too gay,
because you're beautiful, and smart, incredibly talented and oh **so** loving.

Beat.

Flaming, you're just single right now because you just haven't met that person yet that can match you in all those qualities. You deserve a man just as powerful as you. These mothafuckas you've met thus far just aren't on your level.

BOUKIE

And you LA NEGRITA, what happened to you?

LA NEGRITA

Many atimes, we stay in toxic, abusive, tarnished, **dangerous** relationships, because we fear being alone.

Beat.

Boukie, I don't want you to be scared of being alone.

(*LONG PAUSE. All characters process.*)

BOUKIE

(*Looks up at friend.*) Like...what happened to you? At the club?

Beat.

Something is wrong La Negrita. It's written all over your Negress face... You've just changed so much since then. All of a sudden you and BUDDY, JR. won't even look each other in the eyes. You won't talk about it, and I SAW YOU fucking coach!!

(*LA NEGRITA refuses to engage, starts walking away. Getting up gathering things.*)

LA NEGRITA

I don't want to talk about it. What do you want me to say Boukie? I am **unhappy,** okay? I am not happy.

BOUKIE

Why do you let your happiness be determined by **men?** Why do you depend on **men** to be the cause of your happiness? Don't ever let a **man** be the cause of your downfall.

LA NEGRITA

Fuck y'all. (*Starts walking away.*)

BOUKIE

You get drunk, and then you just disappear for days, weeks, **months.**

FLAMING FILIPPE

La Negrita. We're saying this because we're your friends. We don't want anything to happen to you!

LA NEGRITA

(*Starts to laugh hysterically.*) Don't want anything to happen to **me?** BAHAHAH. Well, it's too fuckin late motherfuckers! You **really** want to know what happened at the club? You **really** wanna know what happened to me? BUDDY happened to me. I woke up, bloody, unconscious. Dress ripped with BUDDY on top of me.

BOUKIE

Menina!

LA NEGRITA

So my solution? I fuck. I fuck till I'm numb. I fuck till I no longer feel pleasure or pain. I fuck until they forget my name. I fuck until I forget. Cuz with every fuck, I stop missing Buddy. just a little less. I fuck people I don't even give a fuck about. Cuz that way, I'll never fall in love.

BOUKIE

Menina. (*Consoles friend.*) God menina, I feel terrible, I'm sorry. I had no idea. I had no right to yell at you. It was my fault. I should have been there. I'm your friend. I—

LA NEGRITA

—After what he did to me, why do I still want him? Why is it that we always want the ones who hurt us the most? Maybe I was asking for it.

FLAMING FILIPPE

Dige, 'asking for it'? Menina? What the fuck? What do you mean? It's not your fault!

LA NEGRITA

Maybe...maybe he doesn't remember...Maybe he was too drunk...maybe it was a blackout...Buddy he could never...He would never...There's no way he meant it! He said he loved me...

Beat.

No, maybe it is...Maybe it's the way I dress. Maybe I need a butt reduction...If I had a pancake ass...

FLAMING FILIPPE

Pancake ass?

LA NEGRITA

I have always prefered the aesthetic of the pancake tit!!!!

BOUKIE

This is SERIOUS menina.

LA NEGRITA

Nobody takes me seriously, I'm just a character that people use for their enjoyment.

BOUKIE

YOU don't deserve this. You've been through enough already. You still love white people even when they treat you like shit and you always smile— but I haven't seen that smile in a while. I just— (*Chokes*). Blancos de mierda!!!

LA NEGRITA

How could Buddy have done that to me? I thought he cared about me... Maybe he never cared about me, maybe it was all a scam. Maybe he just pretended to love me.

Beat.

How am I supposed show my face in the caf? Or anywhere on campus? What if I see an athlete... I can never escape!

BOUKIE

Don't worry about that manita. We will cross that bridge when we come to it. WE can go the caf together, you, me, Kiki, Esau, Flaming Felippe, hell, heck, even Mo'nica Vane can come if you want! You're not alone manita. What you need to be concentrating on from here on out, is not settling for these douchebag assholes with these D3 tendencies. You need to stop looking and be found.

Beat.

You're not alone manita. I'm lonely too. I'm searching. But we will be found, and when he/she/they/it comes they will tell us our beauty blows their mind, and stains their soul. They will tell us that without us they are nothing. We made them something.

LA NEGRITA

I miss him even though he hurt me. Every time I think of him I feel pathetic. Because every time I think of him, I'm reminded that he doesn't think of me. But I'm a sick bastard for thinking we are meant to be together eventually.

FLAMING FILIPPE

You're not sick LA NEGRITA, you're just hurting.

LA NEGRITA

But was he always that person all along? Or was I so blinded by love, that I saw what I wanted to see? Or did he fool me into showing me what he wanted me to see?

BOUKIE

People change and it sucks.

LA NEGRITA

I feel like I'll always be alone forever.

Beat.

I feel like my stomach has been filled with asphalt and I've been thrown to the bottom of the sea. I'm drowning, and no one will save me. I'm drowning in his love—except he doesn't love me. Or maybe he did love me. Isn't that what love does? Makes us all a little crazy?

FLAMING FILIPPE

Well sweetie, you're safe now. Mama's gonna take care of this Oppressor for you, don't worry. White people are not worth your tears. White people will never love you as much as you love them...Have I taught you nothing? FUCK white people! They just want your pee to pass drug tests...

LA NEGRITA

Did his mother not teach him to be careful to make a women cry, for God counts her every tear?

FLAMING FILIPPE

I DON'T LIKE UGLY PEOPLE!

LA NEGRITA

Buddy isn't ugly.... (*Awkward silence.*) Is he??

⟦*Beat.*

I just want to have enough faith in the white race that one day I will find my non-oppressor.

BLACKOUT.

Scene VII: KISSLAND

LA NEGRITA

A lot has transpired since Buddy Jr. oppressed me at the club.

I'm still a sad Negress looking for love. (*Makes sad face.*) But it's Boukie's fiesta for her birthday!!!! E'rybody hur. Jerome, Filippe, Mo'nica Vane—Kiki even got special visiting privileges from Nurse Ratchet! I'm just trying to have a good time and get turnt up. I just hope Buddy Jr. doesn't show up uninvited...

LUKE

Hey, you can't leave your coat here.

LA NEGRITA

Okay.

LUKE

I mean. Cuz I live here. The party's downstairs. It's not our floor that's having the party.

LA NEGRITA

Okay, **BYE FELICIA!!!!** (*Grabs coat and goes downstairs.*)

BOUKIE

What was that about?

LA NEGRITA

(*Dances with BOUKIE*) I dunno. Luke's acting funny—he was so damn annoying!

BOUKIE

I know, totally! Let's just dance.

(*VANE approaches ESAU.*)

VANE

Hey.

ESAU

What's good Mo'nica?

VANE

You wanna dance?

ESAU

No.

VANE

Well, why not?

ESAU

(*Looks over at NURSE RATCHET.*) CUZ I AIN'T GOING BACK THERE!!!

VANE

Whatever, I'm too hot.com for these bitches anyways. (*Women on stage get into formation and start twerking to "I'm Out" by Ciara.*)

LA NEGRITA

Totally. Hey Frankie! (*Dances toward FRANKIE. Clearly drunk.*) Wanna dance?

FRANKIE

Naw, I'm not drunk enough to dance.

LA NEGRITA

The hell! You're Trinidadian!

FRANKIE

But I'm not though...

BOUKIE

But I heard your dad was dating one...

FRANKIE

Shhhh. Don't tell the team that.

BOUKIE

Girl, what I know? I'm drunk bitches! Woooooooohhhhhh!!!

NURSE RATCHET

Can everybody stop asking everybody to dance, and just dance already! I need to go home!

(*LA NEGRITA begins twerking on floor.*)

KIKI

Dassit LA NEGRITA! Do the Miley!

(*Approaches LA NEGRITA is LUKE.*)

KIKI

It's my birthday bitches! (*Big Booty Hoe starts to play in background.*)

LUKE

Hey.

LA NEGRITA

I have my coat, look! (*Points to coat.*)

LUKE

I just wanted to know if you maybe wanted to dance?

LA NEGRITA

NIGGAHHHHH!!!

Beat.

I do not wish to dance with you. (*Takes shot of tequila.*)

Beat.

Now... Reclaiming my time. (*Starts twerking.*)

LUKE

Okay. (*Sadly walks away.*)

LA NEGRITA

("*Hideaway*" *by Tessanne Chin starts to play in background. LA NEGRITA really likes this song.*) Well, since you asked so politely. (*Begins to dance with him, then she suddenly vomits on him.*) Oh my God I'm so sorry!!! (*Gets embarrassed.*)

Beat.

I'm so sorry!!!

LUKE

(*Laughs.*) It's okay. Looks wanna use my bathroom? I just live right upstairs. (*Points upward. Looks at her. Waits for her to nod her head.*)

LA NEGRITA

Okay.

LUKE

Okay? (*Outreaches his hand to her. She takes it but only because she can't walk straight. He leads her to his apartment.*)

Beat.

Do you want some water or something?

LA NEGRITA

Ok. (*Starts crying.*)

LUKE

(*Whispers softly.*) Is it okay if I hold you?

LA NEGRITA

(*Looks up.*) Yes. (*They hold each other for a while.*)

LA NEGRITA

Everything hurts.

LUKE

I know.

LA NEGRITA

(*Gets defensive.*) No. you do NOT fuckin know.

LUKE

It means... Nina, I'm on the team.

Beat.

I know what he did to you. I'm sorry he hurt you. I'm sorry I—I'm sorry I couldn't' help you. I'm sorry I couldn't protect you, I'm sorry. I'm sorry, I'm sorry I wasn't—

LA NEGRITA

—enough. (*Whispers to him and places her lips on his mouth to quiet him.*)

LUKE

Nina?

LA NEGRITA

Nina... nobody even calls me that anymore. I almost—I almost forgot that I had a name.

(*Luke kisses her.*)

BLACKOUT.

Scene VIII: I Just Want to Have Enough Faith in the White Race That I Will Find my Non-Oppressor One Day

(*"The Weekend" by SZA plays softly in background. LA NEGRITA hurries out of her art class. In a rush she drops all of her books. LUKE hurries to her rescue. This is the first time they've seen each other since their intimate exchange of words...and saliva.*)

LUKE

Here, you go, I think you dropped these. (*He smiles at her.*)

LA NEGRITA

You think?

LUKE

(*Adjusts glasses.*) I'm sorry?

LA NEGRITA

Nothing.

LUKE

No, really, what did you say?

Beat.

"You think."

LA NEGRITA

(*Continues with her attitude.*) If you heard what I said, why did you ask me to repeat it? (*Snatches sketchpad from his hand.*) Thank you. (*Sarcastically*).

LUKE

Just trying to help. (*Luke notices LA NEGRITA glaring at him. He feels like he's seeing her for the first time.*) You seem upset.

LA NEGRITA

Oh, what, are you a psych major? (*Sarcasm.*)

LUKE

Actually— (*Adjusts snapback.*)

LA NEGRITA

I don't care what your major is. (Blushes.) I really should be going. (*Tries to grab her things and hurry past him but drops her backpack clumsily in an effort to escape. LUKE and LA NEGRITA bob simultaneously to grab LA NEGRITA's knapsack. They bump heads.*)

LA NEGRITA

Aye coño!

LUKE

What?

LA NEGRITA

Nothing. Really, I have to go... (*More attitude.*)

LUKE

Why are you always in such a rush?

BEAT

Was that Spanish?

BEAT

Are you Spanish?

LA NEGRITA

What's with the 21 questions, Fifty Cent? (Smirks.)

LUKE

Fifty Cents?

LA NEGRITA

Well, I really must go. (*Rolls eyes.*)

LUKE

(*Holds her hand briefly out of reflex.*) Hey, what's with the attitude? I was just trying to help.

LA NEGRITA

(*Mockingly silently mimics him. Notices his hand on hers, but doesn't flinch. She blushes. They make eye contact; she turns away as he gazes into her eyes.*)

LUKE

(*Gets up from ground as well.*) About the other night... (*Looks at LA NEGRITA with concern, but also at awe of her exotic beauty, mocha skin, piercing eyes, full lips and the way her hips don't lie.*)

LA NEGRITA

(*Says softly to him as the continue to look to each other.*) I just really think I should go.

LUKE

(*Scratches his hair.*) Well, can you at least walk me to my next class?

LA NEGRITA

No... I will NOT walk you to your next class. The fuck?

LUKE

Wait, wait, that's not what I meant!

Beat.

What I was trying to say is, can I walk you to your next class?

LA NEGRITA

No, thank you.

LUKE

You just make me very nervous.

LA NEGRITA

So you kiss me and NOW **you're** nervous.

LUKE

(*Laughs uncomfortably.*) I was drunk.

Beat.

I'm very sorry.

LA NEGRITA

Good day. (*Starts to walk away.*)

LUKE

(*Fumbles hands through hair.*) I just get nervous talking to girls...Especially girls like you.

LA NEGRITA

Girls like me? (*Gathers things and tries to rush past him.*) Now, what the hell is that supposed to mean?

LUKE

Why are you so damn defensive?! Maybe I just want to get to know you?

LA NEGRITA

Why? That's what you do? Kiss a girl, let them feel all vulnerable, spend the night—

LUKE

Look, I'm sorry. I just—

Beat.

I dunno. There's something about you.

LA NEGRITA

What? That I'm a thot?

LUKE

No.

Beat.

You are not a thot.

Beat.

It's just—you're just not the kind of person someone forgets.

LA NEGRITA

What do you mean? (*Places hands on hips.*)

LUKE

I don't remember many things, like about last night. I don't really remember. And I'm sorry.

Beat.

But your eyes...they're something I always remember. They're like—like the difference between being pierced by ice water cold knives or being immersed in a frothing pool of perfectly warm water.

BEAT

With bubbles.

BEAT

They are love and hate at the same time.

LA NEGRITA

Poetry is not your strong suit. **Please** stick to hockey.

LUKE

I feel insulted. (*Places hand on chest, mocking being wounded. LA NEGRITA giggles, pushes hair behind her ear.*)

Beat.

So, wanna meet up sometime?

LA NEGRITA

Perhaps.

BLACKOUT.

Scene IX: The Coffee Shop (Since All Great Plays Seem to Have One)

(Broken Pussy by Issa Rae plays as a transition song.)

LA NEGRITA

(Addresses audience.) So I've decided to meet Luke at the Coffee Shop. He wants to talk, or something. I dunno, I've decided to give him a chance I guess. I mean, I've never had anybody talk to me the way that Luke did. *(Looks at LUKE.)* Is this my seat? *(Points to only other chair at coffee table.)*

LUKE

Of course it is. *(Gives big cheesy smile.)*

LA NEGRITA

Well, aren't you **prompt?**

LUKE

Is that not cool?! *(Says worried.)*

LA NEGRITA

(Acknowledges that he is trying to impress her.) No, no, it's fine! *(She smiles.)*

LUKE

So, do you like Triple K?

LA NEGRITA

(Puzzled because nobody has ever asked her that question before.) What?

LUKE

Our school. Do you like our school?

LA NEGRITA

Is that even a serious question? *(Quietly looks down and stirs drink.)*

LUKE

What?

LA NEGRITA

No.

Beat.

I do NOT like Triple K.

LUKE

Oh well... (*Scratches head.*) Why do you go here?

LA NEGRITA

I wanted to be different, I guess... but the same.

LUKE

What?

LA NEGRITA

Never mind.

LUKE

You wanted to be different by going somewhere that you hate?

LA NEGRITA

Never mind. Forget about it. (*Changes subject.*) So why do you go here? To skate around a rink?

LUKE

I wouldn't call it "skating around a rink". It's called "hockey" and it's a sport.

Beat.

Sorry it's not soccer, or basketball or whatever. Baseball! (*Points up to painting of baby girl hanging in coffee shop.*) And, as a matter of fact, I also paint.

LA NEGRITA

(*In awe of painting.*) You did this? You drew this? Wow, you're really good.

Beat.

But I'm better.

LUKE

Of course you are. (*Smiles.*) I Like your voice.

LA NEGRITA

What?

Beat

You've heard me sing? (*Looks embarrassed.*)

Beat.

When have you heard me sing?

LUKE

At the gym.

Beat.

You work at the gym. I hear you singing there all the time. You have a beautiful voice.

LA NEGRITA

Wow.

LUKE

(*Raises eyebrows.*) What?

LA NEGRITA

That's what you notice about me?

LUKE

Yeah...

LA NEGRITA

That's not what the team notices.

LUKE

Yeah, I **hear** the locker room talk, but I **listen to** your voice.

Beat.

They're jocks, what do you expect? (*Takes another sip of his drink.*) You have a beautiful voice.

Beat.

(*Changes subject.*) So, what's your favorite tv show?

LA NEGRITA

What's **your** favorite tv show? Real Husbands of Hollywood?

LUKE

I asked **you** first. (*Takes sip of coffee.*)

Beat.

Curb your enthusiasm.

LA NEGRITA

Excuse me!? You know what, then **fuck** you nigga. You racist. You better check yourself before talking to me like that—

LUKE

What did I say?

LA NEGRITA

"Curb your enthusiasm"! That's how you speak to women when you're out on a date.

LUKE

NINA... 'Curb Your Enthusiasm'...it's the name of show.

LA NEGRITA

Oh. (*Shit gets quiet, and VERY awkward.*)

LUKE

(*Laughs it off. Touches her hand.*) It's okay, really.

Beat.

What's **your** favorite movie? (*Changes subject again.*)

LA NEGRITA

Why do you care about tv so much?

LUKE

I'm a coach potato.

LA NEGRITA

Well, you're white so—

LUKE

—Just kidding! I'm a visual arts major you silly little girl.

LA NEGRITA

Oh, well in that case...Lakeview Terrace... my favorite movie is definitely Lake View Terrace.

LUKE

Lakeview Terrace?!

LA NEGRITA

Yea. (*Laughs.*)

Beat.

Have you seen it before?

LUKE

Yeah, I've seen that before. (*Chuckles.*) Is that the movie with Samuel L. Jackson and uhhh Kerry Washington?

LA NEGRITA

That's the one.

LUKE

Oh man, Kerry Washington.

LA NEGRITA

(*Gets a tad jealous.*) What about Kerry Washington? (*Says softly.*)

LUKE

She's an incredible actress.

LA NEGRITA

(*Taken aback.*) Wow.

LUKE

What?

LA NEGRITA

Kerry Washington.

LUKE

What?

BEAT.

You didn't think I'd know who Kerry Washington is?

LA NEGRITA

No, it's not that. (*Looks taken aback.*)

LUKE

What is it then?

LA NEGRITA

I'm just surprised...

LUKE

That I've watched Lakeview Terrace? I watch 'BET' sometimes...

LA NEGRITA

Luke, it's pronounced B-E-T... awkward...I never met a man who described Kerri Washington as a great actress.

LUKE

She is! (*Gets defensive about his views on Kerry Washington.*)

LA NEGRITA

(*Extends her hand on top of his.*) No, usually when I say Kerry Washington the first thing a guy says to describe her is "sexy".

LUKE

Well, she is sexy, she's equally as talented as actress. 'I Think I Love My Wife' did not serve her any justice.

(*Long pause.*)

LA NEGRITA

(*Looks mischievous.*) Do you think **I'm** sexy? (*Points out outfit. Gives him mischievous look.*)

LUKE

Now, Nina. Why you gotta do that? We're talking about the damn movie.

LA NEGRITA

There's sex in the movie!

LUKE

And that's why it's your favorite?

LA NEGRITA

Yup! Exactly. That and the fact that Patrick Wilson is oh so sexy.

LUKE

Right.

LA NEGRITA

What!?

LUKE

Bullshit.

LA NEGRITA

What's bullshit?

LUKE

(*Looks deep in her eyes.*) That can't be why it's your favorite movie. (*Says quietly.*)

LA NEGRITA

You know what's bullshit? It's bullshit when I say "Kerry Washington" the first thing you say is "great actress."

LUKE

She is!

LA NEGRITA

Whatever, Fitz

LUKE

Fitz? Who the hell is Fitz!

LA NEGRITA

You're so white! Don't you watch Scandal?

LUKE

I don't even have cable...

LA NEGRITA

But you just said you watch BET!

LUKE

Well yeah, I lied.

LA NEGRITA

Why?

LUKE

To impress you.

LA NEGRITA

Whether you have cable or not isn't going to impress me. What impresses me is the fact that you asked me out. Here. (*Mood changes.*)

Beat.

So, why is it that I like the movie? (*Mockingly.*) You tell **me** why **I** like the movie.

LUKE

You like the movie because you are a hopeless romantic. You believe in love above all, no matter the circumstance.

LA NEGRITA

No, LUKE, that's not why I enjoy the movie. I'm cynical, okay? Samuel L. Jackson saw that interracial relations were the devil and tried to **DESTROY** them.

LUKE

Are we talking about Samuel L. Jackson that actor, or Abel Turner the character? Cuz Samuel L. Jackson's wife is white...

LA NEGRITA

No, she isn't!

LUKE

She isn't?

LA NEGRITA

She isn't!

LUKE

Does this mean the dates over?

LA NEGRITA

I dunno.

LUKE

I hit a chord, didn't I?

LA NEGRITA

I'm not a piano.

LUKE

Why is everything so black and white with you?

LA NEGRITA

Enough with the piano!

LUKE

It is! You see everything through race.

LA NEGRITA

How can I not? You know what you are to me? You are my savior and my oppressor.

LUKE

What the fuck is that?

LA NEGRITA

You are. You're both.

LUKE

Bullshit. I'm neither. I'm me.

(*Pause, biddies shake heads.*)

Beat.

I just can't be this white guy to you. (*Pause.*) Everybody is looking for love. Some people just don't have the balls to admit it.

LA NEGRITA

(*Looks at him. Long pause.*) Luke, why am I here? Why do you... why do you like me. (*Says softly.*)

LUKE

I dunno. I just care about you, okay? I'm part of the team—and I wasn't there to protect you from BUDDY, I wasn't there to stop them, and I feel guilty. Not because of any complex, but because—ugh, I just care, okay? I care what happens to you.

LA NEGRITA

Care about me? You don't care about me! You don't even know me.

LUKE

I don't know you. But what I **do** know is that you've been loving men who treat you like you're ordinary. And you're FAR from ordinary. You're extraordinary. You are **REMARKABLE.** (*Places his hand on hers. Intertwines his fingers in hers.*)

LA NEGRITA

(*He looks at her. She looks back.*) What?

LUKE

(*Smiles at her.*) We're holding hands. (LA NEGRITA looks around.) In public.

LA NEGRITA

(*Widens eyes.*) We gon get lynched!

LUKE

Shut up.

(*They kiss.*)

BLACKOUT.

Scene X: WITCH BITCH

(*BOUKIE enters VANE's dorm room to get hair done. Room is decorated with crystals, incense, wigs, and dolls. Sade is playing softly in background, sage is burning.*)

VANE

It's a full moon.

BOUKIE

Yeah. (*Looks around Vane's room.*)

Beat.

I always forget how weird you are. *(VANE lights up a blunt.)*

Beat.

Hey, are you even allowed to do that in here?

VANE

I'm an R-A—I do whatever the fuck I want.

BOUKIE

Okay, fair. (*Takes hit of blunt.*)

VANE

(*Takes out crystal ball. Begins tinkering with it.*) Boo, what troubles you so? I see a cloud above your head. And hate in your head. (*Points to smoke shapes that form from cigarette smoke.*)

BOUKIE

It's really nothing.

VANE

(*Reaches out to touch friend's third eye.*) Tell me.

BOUKIE

(*Whispers.*) It's La Negrita.

VANE

(*Mood changes.*) I'm all kumbaya, but it's enough to cut a bitch off. What did that **retard** do now?

BOUKIE

Do you even know why she's coming over to get her hair done?

VANE

Self Care Sunday?

BOUKIE

Um, no.

VANE

Full moon ritual?

BOUKIE

Still incorrect.

VANE

Hmmmm, voodoo doll?

BOUKIE

Um, no Vane. (*Says under breath.*) My friends are **so** fuckin' weird.

VANE

(*Stands.*) She's going out on a date?

Beat.

Already?

BOUKIE

It's like, the world revolves around La Negrita, and we're just character's living in it.

Beat.

It hasn't even been a month since Fight Club, and she's already moving on to another nigga?

VANE

Well, maybe that's the only way she knows how to heal and move on.

BOUKIE

By sucking a dick? (*Laughs.*) Because we **all** fuckin know La Negrita. She just falls for these oppressors that oppress the fuck all over her heart.

VANE

Boukie—

BOUKIE

I heard she's going to the Ranger Rewards.

VANE

What?!

Beat.

The athletic banquet?!

BOUKIE

Yes girl.

VANE

I hope she doesn't get hurt.

BOUKIE

At this point, I don't even care what happens to La Negrita. She just keeps setting herself up for this shit to happen.

VANE

Maybe it's too soon to jump into something like that. (*BOUKIE and VANE pause to think.*)

BOUKIE

Please tell me. Why do any of us take her shit? Like, why the fuck do we even bother keeping her around?

VANE

Because La Negrita is each of us. La Negrita is all of us. She is what we wish we could be. Naïve and just carefree. Blind and forgiving of the harsh realities of our worlds.

Beat.

Or maybe it's that despite anything, she is **always** uncontrollably herself. Despite all her damage, she still has the ability to see the best in everybody she encounters.

Beat.

And you know, she's strong. She just doesn't show it—or maybe she just doesn't **know** it.

Beat.

And you know what? There's nothing stronger than allowing yourself to be in love. (*BOUKIE and VANE pause to think again.*)

BOUKIE

I should go.

LA NEGRITA

(*Mood changes once LA NEGRITA enters room.*) BOUKIE! (*Runs to friend for embrace. BOUKIE walks away.*)

BOUKIE

I have to go.

LA NEGRITA

(*Smiling.*) But Boukie, I just got here!

BOUKIE

I really should go. Bye La Negrita. (*Kisses VANE on forehead, picks up helmet and shoves past Negrita to walk away.*)

LA NEGRITA

But where are you going?

BOUKIE

Reclaiming my time.

LA NEGRITA

(*Turns to VANE*) What was that all about?

VANE

What is **this** all about? (*Looks around at salon.*) Why do you want to change your hair?

LA NEGRITA

I dunno, I just wanted something more palpable... you know, more conformative.

VANE

What do you mean?

LA NEGRITA

You know, I was just thinking about getting some straight back tracks... All this hair just gets me too much attention. So maybe we can try a relaxer or Brazilian blowout—

VANE

I don't get it. What's wrong with your hair?

LA NEGRITA

I just... I just need a change, you know? Try something different. Less distracting.

VANE

Yes, but I don't understand why you're trying to change your hair manita.

LA NEGRITA

It's just that Lukie asked me to the banquet—

VANE

Lukie? (*Dies of laughter.*) For the life of me I can't comprehend how pink penis can get you so dickmatized girl.

LA NEGRITA

I am not dickmatized, asshole!

VANE

La Negrita, in all seriousness, what are you going to do tomorrow?

LA NEGRITA

(*Rolls eyes.*) Go to a banquet tomorrow, the hell?

VANE

Ohhhh manita, manita, manita. You see... but you do not **see.**

Beat.

Manita, what does our future hold?

LA NEGRITA

I don't—

VANE

Take a minute. Pause. Think. (*Some time passes.*)

LA NEGRITA

Mo'nica, I realized...I never really thought that far.

VANE

That is your problem menita. We all have our futures mapped out. I'm going into holistic healing, Kiki's going to law school, Esau is joining the army, heck even Buddy got his future paved out for him.

Beat.

(*Speaks softly and gently.*) Manita, we are only saying these things because we want the best for you. A man hurt you and I just...I don't want the actions of one man to stagnant your whole future. We are brown beautiful intelligent indigenous mamis. Our purpose it to be resilient. Rise up. Your ancestors and spirit guides never doubt the infinite possibility over your life, so you just stop sucking pink dick.

(*KIKI enters.*)

KIKI

What is **this** all about? (*Looks around at VANE's room*). Why did you bring me here?

LA NEGRITA

(*Smiles.*) So, we never really got to talk since you got out, so I thought maybe we could get our hair done together?

KIKI

You are **so** fuckin naïve...

LA NEGRITA

What?

KIKI

Negrita, **now** you want to talk about me and the institute? After you let **all** this time past by without sayin **shit?**

Beat.

And you **KNOW** black girls don't get haircuts.

LA NEGRITA

Now Kiki, that's your problem! You just have to be more open minded! Like me! (*Smiles.*)

KIKI

Who got you all dickmatized?

LA NEGRITA

KIKI!

KIKI

Am I wrong?

LA NEGRITA

Kiki, must you be so crude? I am NOT dickmatized. And His name is Luke. (*Beams.*)

KIKI

He sounds white.

LA NEGRITA

It doesn't matter.

KIKI

You just **don't** know how to be alone. Do you?

LA NEGRITA

What?

KIKI

LA NEGRITA, since I've known you, you have **never** been alone. There's always another boy. You always have a friend.

Beat.

But Nina, until you have been happy alone with yourself, how can you truly ever be happy with someone new? (*Allow time to let sink in.*)

LA NEGRITA

He invited me to the Athletic Banquet!

KIKI

What?! (*Snaps at her.*)

LA NEGRITA

Hey, que paso?

KIKI

The athletic banquet is the epitome of oppression! That's when all the athletes find their colored target and run a train all over her.

Beat.

They'll roofie you. Hell, they might even lynch ya!

LA NEGRITA

Don't scare me. Coach will be there...

(KIKI *laughs in disbelief*)

LA NEGRITA

(*Ignoring KIKI and addressing attention back to VANE.*) Luke will be there...

KIKI

And? (*Looks at LA NEGRITA and laughs.*) Is he gonna protect you like Buddy did?

Beat.

Negrita, you **do** understand Buddy will be there...right?

Beat.

When are you going to learn to save yourself? Because me, Boukie, Esau, Filippe, Vane (*points to VANE*) we're not going to be here forever menina. So you **really,** menina, you **really** need to think about what you want.

LA NEGRITA

(*Says softly.*) I want to get my hair done, that's what I want.

KIKI

Typical.

LA NEGRITA

What?

KIKI

Typical Negrita. I just find it very hard to believe that you can be so damn complacent. Go ahead, get your hair done. While you're at it, please gather some ambition and a 5-year plan.

Beat.

I'm leaving. (*Gets up to leave LA NEGRITA like BOUKIE did.*)

LA NEGRITA

I don't understand your problem KIKI!

KIKI

(*Tone changes. Faces LA NEGRITA).* La Negrita, do you understand if I was in a crisis, you wouldn't be the person I would call?

LA NEGRITA

KIKI, I—

KIKI

You what? Don't know how to be a good friend? Only know how to suck dick?

LA NEGRITA

Kiki where is all this coming from?

KIKI

It's coming from—

Beat.

You were my person La Negrita. My **person.** I was in trouble. I needed your help. I **called** you to the institute to save me. And you left me to save myself.

Beat.

You were my person La Negrita, and I watched you leave with the enemy...you went to Buddy with open arms. You never once turned back. You didn't even **try** to save me. You were **compliant.** Nurse Ratchet asked you to leave and **you just did.**

Beat.

God. You didn't even fight for me.

LA NEGRITA

I didn't think you needed saving.

KIKI

Why? Because I'm Machine Gun Kiki? I'm the **strong** friend who's always saving herself? Always saving everybody else?

Beat.

Well, LA NEGRITA sometimes I **need** saving, and I never have anybody so I always have to save my fucking self. I'm always over here fighting for everybody else. It would be nice to know I have someone out there fighting for me.

Beat.

You fucking left me in prison. Who am I? Gandhi? Mandela?

LA NEGRITA

Kiki, but why won't you **ever** take responsibility for your own shit. Why is it **always** white people?! For Heaven's **sake** Kiki, just grow up.

KIKI

You know what La Negrita, it used to be white people I felt bad for. But it's you. And you know why? One day you will **finally** realize that white people will **NEVER** love you as much as you love them.

LA NEGRITA

(*Wounded.*) Kiki, what happened to us? You're my—you're my best friend.

KIKI

You know, sometimes the more you get to know someone, the more you love them. And then sometimes, it's just the complete opposite.

Beat.

I guess that's what is with love. When you love someone, you just see what you want to see. Not the reality of things. And La Negrita, after **all** this time, I'm **finally** seeing you for who you really are—a disappointment. (*KIKI and VANE get up and walk away from LA NEGRITA like BOUKIE had. LA NEGRITA is left alone.*)

BLACKOUT.

Scene XI: Trust Issues

(*"Don't Touch My Hair" by Solange is playing in the background. LUKE is pacing impatiently for LA NEGRITA to take her to the banquet. LA NEGRITA rushes in.*)

LUKE

Nina, where the hell have you been?!

LA NEGRITA / LUKE

I— / Hurry up, we're late!

LUKE

I still gotta put gas in the car, pick my parents up from the airport. Get the booze for the boys.

LA NEGRITA

(*Stalls him.*) Wait bae.

LUKE

What?

(*Long pause.*)

LA NEGRITA

(*Goes over to kiss him.*)

LUKE

That was nice. (*Smiles. And kisses her back.*) Okay, we can't do this right now.

LA NEGRITA

(*Flirts with him.*) Whyyyy?? (*Bats eyelashes.*)

LUKE

(*Chuckles.*) Because we're late.

LA NEGRITA

Wait!

LUKE

What now? (*Looks at her puzzled.*)

LA NEGRITA

You look so handsome!

LUKE

Tha—

LA NEGRITA

Let me take a picture!!! (*Rummages through purse to retrieve phone.*) Instagram! (*Looks at pic she took.*) My bae is so handsome! #mce

LUKE

Okay, Nina, you look—

LA NEGRITA

This tie! (*Runs over to play with his tie.*) This tie looks sooo good on you!

Beat.

It just really...you know? It **really** brings out the color of your eyes.

LUKE / LA NEGRITA

Nina— / Your hair, so handsome! (*Plays with hair.*)

LUKE

(*Grabs hands sternly, looks into her eyes.*) Okay, I look really nice, but I will look so much better with you next to me. So, let's go.

LA NEGRITA

Like this? (*Says softly, points to hair.*)

LUKE

(*Looks at her.*) Yeah, you look beautiful, hurry up, let's go!

LA NEGRITA

Ahh—

LUKE

(*Interrupts her excitedly.*) This is my big day, Nina! I'm getting the Kim, Kanye, Kevin University Ranger award for most valuable playa—

LA NEGRITA

—Luke—

LUKE

—my parents are gonna be there Nina! This is so exciting! I can't wait for them to meet you! And ohhhhhhhh man, when the team sees how beautiful you look. (*Smiles.*) It's our senior year Nina! The beginning of the rest of our lives begins tonight!

LA NEGRITA

(*Thinks about her future. **Her** future. This is the first time she thinks about the future.*) Beautiful?! Luke, do you see me?!

Beat.

(*Sits on couch. Face in her palms. Long face, thinking.*)

LUKE

(*Takes one look at her ratchet hair.*) Yeah, you look BEAUTIFUL! (*Says genuinely.*)

LA NEGRITA

How can you even say that?

LUKE

Nina, what are you talking about?

LA NEGRITA

I'm not going.

LUKE

What?

LA NEGRITA

I said I'm not going.

LUKE

What do you **mean** you're not **going?!** (*Takes off glasses to look at her.*)

LA NEGRITA

You heard me. Look.

Beat.

I saysssssssss. IIIIIIIIIIIIIIIII'm, noooooooooooot, going!!!

LUKE / LA NEGRITA

What the hell? / LUKE—

LUKE

NINA, what the hell are you talking about? Let's go. (*Pulls her hand to leave.*)

LA NEGRITA

(*Drops hand.*) No LUKE, I'm not going anywhere.

LUKE

What, what is this?

LA NEGRITA

I'm not going anywhere with my hair looking like this. (*Says under breath.*)
It's ratchet. My tracks are all hanging by the edge of glory and shit...

LUKE

I don't even know what that means...

Beat.

I told you, you look fine. What are you...?

LA NEGRITA

I'm ugly Luke! Look at me! Look at my weave! I look ratchet! Luke, I am
UGLY. I'm not going.

LUKE

Belky, please (*Says softly.*) Don't do this. (*Holds her hands.*)

LA NEGRITA

(*Shouts.*) Are you blind!? Look at my weave! The tracks are loose. My braids
are showing. The tracks aren't tight enough. She used hot pink thread! The
textures don't match. This is a 4 when I'm clearly a 1B. It's too short. The
lengths are not consistent. My edges aren't smooth. It's stiff. It's stale. It
smells bad. This weave is used hair! This isn't even human hair...synthetic
is pathetic! (Scoffs.) It doesn't look natural...some hair is sewed, some is
glued, some is CLAMPED. It's stringy. This is KINKY hair! Not Brazilian,
not INDIAN, not Peruvian, not MALAYSIAN. I look like a motha fuckin
AFRICANUS!!!! My weave is SHEDDING. My new growth is out of control.
I look like a helmet head. I look like a freakin shaggy dog! This is the LAST
time I let a white bitch do me up!

LUKE

(*Sits next to LA NEGRITA.*) Nina, what's gotten into you? 'White people
do me up', you never talk like that.

LA NEGRITA

Well, I was just with Boukie and Kiki, and they just made a lot of sense about a lot of things, that's all. (*Crosses arms and looks away from him.*)

Beat.

I've realized...before tonight I never really thought about my future. We're graduating tomorrow...and I'm scared.

LUKE

Well Nina, this isn't about you right now.

Beat.

I'm really sorry, it's about me...my banquet, my parents flying **all the way** from Canada to see me.

Beat.

To see us.

LA NEGRITA

How can you even talk about us?

Beat.

I've spent all this time thinking about us. And not enough time thinking about **my** future.

Beat.

Luke, you know what you're doing after tomorrow...I mean did ever once think to ask me?

LUKE

Baby, I would love to be your life coach, but not right now.

Beat.

My parents—

LA NEGRITA

—Canada isn't far.

LUKE

NINA—

LA NEGRITA

They didn't have to take a plane.

LUKE

So are we leaving now?

LA NEGRITA

I can't go.

LUKE

For the love of—

LA NEGRITA

I can't!

LUKE

Nina, really? Are we REALLY doing this right now?

LA NEGRITA

(*Takes heels off.*)

LUKE

You will sabotage anything good that's standing right in front of you.

Beat.

NINA, once I walk out that door. I'm gone, do you understand that?

LA NEGRITA

I'M UGLY!!!!!!!!

Beat.

And I'm scared. And I'm damaged. And I'm lost...but mostly just scared. I've been so scared this whole time, that I never once took the time to think about my future...instead I've just been distracted myself with relationships.

Beat.

I've been distracting myself with you, with Boukie, Kiki, Vane, Esau...they call me selfish, yet... I haven't really thought about myself.

Beat.

I should have been more selfish. If I was more selfish maybe I would know what I'm going to do tomorrow...like you.

LUKE

Listen, Nina. Let's just not worry about tomorrow, okay? Let's worry about tonight.

Beat.

Babe, if I'm good, **you're** good. We're a team baby. You're my partner. I got you. I promise, okay? I understand that you're scared. I empathize deeply with you babe.

Beat.

You're beautiful. It doesn't matter what you wear, or **how you do your stupid weaves,** or the color of your skin, you're beautiful.

Beat.

It doesn't matter how you look; I just want you to be there on the most important day of my athletic career.

LA NEGRITA

(*Mumbles under breath.*) You're D3....

LUKE

(*Snaps.*) My one button! you pushed it!

Beat.

I don't have time for this Belky. I'm leaving. (*Heads towards door.*)

LA NEGRITA

That's the way it's got to be? (*These words stop him at doorway.*)

LUKE

Please come with me Nina. I don't care, we're already late. I'll wait for you...I just really want you to come with me.

LA NEGRITA

No, look! (*Point in mirror at her reflection.*) I can't do it.

LUKE

So what, you don't love me?

LA NEGRITA

That's not it.

LUKE

You don't. You don't love me, you don't love yourself. And always hiding behind this damn race bullshit! If you can't look into the mirror and say you love yourself, regardless of how bad you **think** you look, how can you possibly love me?

LA NEGRITA / LUKE

LUKE, what are you— / You don't love me—

LA NEGRITA / LUKE

It has NOTHING— / Prove it.

LA NEGRITA

Prove what?

LUKE

That you love me.

LA NEGRITA

How?

LUKE

I shouldn't have to be the one to tell you that. **That** is just something you should know for yourself. (*LUKE* grabs keys, heads towards door.)

LA NEGRITA

How can you love me Luke? How? We barely know each other. How can you love me Luke? I barely love myself and have absolutely no idea what I want to do the rest of my life, yet alone tomorrow. I'm scared okay?

LUKE

(*Does an about face.*) What do you want from me?

LA NEGRITA

I want you to stay...

LUKE

(*Faces her.*) You want me to stay here...with you? You want me to not go to my award ceremony?

   Beat.

(*LA NEGRITA nods*) Everything is always about you Nina. No, I'm going.

LA NEGRITA

I don't want to embarrass **us**.

LUKE

(*Grabs her shoulders.*) There is absolutely nothing wrong with you! Okay? Why baby? Why can't you see that? There is nothing wrong with you! We are all scared. Half of the people walking past the stage tomorrow have no clue who the fuck they are or where the fuck they're going. Welcome to being a millennium honey.

LA NEGRITA

YOU DON'T UNDERSTAND, YOU'LL NEVER UNDERSTAND!!!!

LUKE

You're right. I don't understand. I thought I did. But I don't.

LA NEGRITA

Another girl.

LUKE / LA NEGRITA

What? / There's another girl.

LUKE

Nina, now what the **fuck** are you even talking about?!

LA NEGRITA

There's **always** another girl.

LUKE

(*Calms himself.*) No Nina, there's no other girl. It's you. It's always been you. It **will** always be you. Even when I walk through that door, it will be you. (*Cups his hands around her.*)

LA NEGRITA

How can you love me but not care about my future?

LUKE

I have. (*Places Varsity ring in her hand and leaves.*)

LA NEGRITA

(*Sobs.*) It's perfect.

(*Lights off, lights on. "Asylum" by John Legend plays loudly in the background.*)

LA NEGRITA

What do you see when you look at me? Do you see strong, do you see weak? (*KIKI approaches stage with chair.*) Women of color are supposed to overcome obstacles of any kind, no matter the circumstance. (*BOUKIE approaches stage with chair.*) And the fact of the matter is, women of color, are WOMEN, which means we are human. (*VANE approaches stage with chair.*) I'm human. (*ESAU approaches stage with chair.*) I do not possess any superhuman strength that makes us able to survive the impossible.

   Beat.

Falling in love makes me afraid of ever falling in love again. What am I afraid of? Falling in love and not being loved back. Because that's what happened. It wasn't a break-up. It was worse. He didn't break my heart. What he did was far more detrimental. He said he didn't.

   Beat.

Even.

   Beat.

Want it.

   Beat.

It was a test trial even before he gave me a chance. There was no warning. I simply just fell in love. And when I fell, I fell hard. And there wasn't anyone there to pick me up. I was alone. I didn't know that was love? Being alone? And no matter how hard I try, the tears just keep coming. They keep falling like I fell. And nobody is there to pick them up. The tears cloud my judgment and I continue to think of him. (*BUDDY approaches stage.*) He hurt me and disguised it as love.

   Beat.

It feels like I will never smile again and mean it. I just feel numb. Numb and scared. And hesitant to be myself. Hesitant to ever let anybody enter my life again. People come and go so easily. I am nothing but disposable to them. Maybe I'm just unlovable. But I'm going to accept this fact now and stay away from any poor imitation of love.

Beat.

I feel as though you can never mend a broken heart. Every time you get your heart broken, the person responsible keeps a little part. Well, I've had my heart broken so many times by so many different people, I think he took the last part. Now I have no heart. Loving him is by no means something I chose to do. I didn't just wake up in the middle of the night and decide to love you. (*LUKE* approaches stage.)

Beat.

(*FRANKIE approaches stage with stool. Seats LA NEGRITA.*) Women of color usually have no happy ending. (*NURSE RATCHET approaches stage and equips LA NEGRITA with a straight jacket.*) My grandmother did not, her mother did not, MY mother did not, I WILL not. I will not. I will...not.

(Pause. LA NEGRIT looks at us. Not at all sure.)

BLACKOUT.

Chapter 8
A Lovely Day | Winifred Summer

W inifred Summer is a first-generation American of Haitian descent who is forever grateful for the many sacrifices her parents made so she could be in the land of opportunity! Winifred found that during her time in the workforce that opportunities were not always welcoming and there appeared to be a rising trend of toxicity in the workplace. Her concerns for people met with challenges in the workforce led her to change her career from health administration to human resources where she proudly advocates and inspires people to have healthy fulfilling careers.

A Lovely Day

I am a dream to life

From ancestors who never laid eyes

On me

Or even heard me speak

A product of sacrifice

Blood

Tears

Sweat

Long hours

Love

Preservation

And labor pains

A dream

A dream that never left the mind

And never made its way out of lips

Until time aligned and possibilities shinned visible

Heroic men and women

Be it plane, foot, or tugboat

Risked it all for me

When no one knew me but God, and

the paths to bring me to earth hadn't even yet crossed

And so I am a destiny fulfilled even in imperfection

Though some may pick me apart

Deflecting.

Distracted.

I have enacted scenes

From the dreams of generations passed

And when I wave my Haitian flag and American flag,

twist around my hand and spin it like a helicopter

It is because I know my presence is bigger than me

And I am so that others can be

I am a day many prayed for, in human form

And with me I carry pieces of the future

Hallelujah

And amen

For this feature

on this masterpiece of a sphere

Called earth

Through prayer

With purpose beyond understanding

A sparkling, beautiful, brown, curvy, unfiltered work

Appreciated by generations down the line

That I may never know

But are known, all in time

www.ingramcontent.com/pod-product-compliance
Lightning Source LLC
Chambersburg PA
CBHW061523050726
47503CB00015B/2685